RESCUE

RESCUE

Stephen O'Connor

HARMONY BOOKS / NEW YORK

Acknowledgments

Some of the stories in this book originally appeared in *The Quarterly*, and a selection from "A Current in the Earth" was first published in *Hubbub*. "A Current in the Earth" is a fictionalized account of John Wesley Powell's 1869 exploration of the Colorado River and the Grand Canyon, based on Powell's own account, *Expedition of the Colorado River of the West and Its Tributaries* (1875); Jack Sumner's memoir quoted in *Colorado River Controversies* (1932), attributed to R.B. Stanton but probably written by J.M. Chalfant; and *Powell of the Colorado* (1951) by William Culp Darrah. Powell's two "inspirational geology" talks are composed largely of only slightly altered quotes from his astonishing descriptions of the Grand Canyon's geological history. The anecdotes put into the mouth of Billy Dunn are based on episodes in Jack Sumner's memoir and preserve a few of Sumner's more colorful turns of phrase.

I would like to thank Yaddo and the Cummington Community of the Arts for providing the peace and comfort that nourish inspiration; my agent, Kim Witherspoon, for her hard work and unfailing enthusiasm; my good friends Rob Murphy, for first inviting me to "Randolph's Party," Bill Logan, and Rob Cohen for their generosity with their time and their excellent criticism; and finally, I would like to thank Helen Benedict, my wife and first reader, without whose love, advice, and support this book could never have been written.

Published by Harmony Books, a division of Crown Publishers, Inc., 225 Park Avenue South, New York, New York 10003.

HARMONY and colophon are trademarks of Crown Publishers, Inc.

Printed in the U.S.A.

Library of Congress Cataloging-in-Publication Data

O'Connor, Stephen.
    Rescue / Stephen O'Connor.
      p.   cm.
    I. Title.
PS3565.C65R4   1989
813'.54—dc19   88-38382
                                                                                  CIP

Book design by Jennifer Harper

ISBN 0-517-57203-6
10 9 8 7 6 5 4 3 2 1

First Edition

To Helen

Contents

I

Help   3
The Afterlife of Lytton Swain   7
Nobody   24

II

Dad; or the Builder of Bridges   47
The Invitation   54
What Makes You Think You Deserve This?   63

III

Loyal Channa   71
The Only Life   96
Lost Goodness   109
Saint Corentin and the Fish   122

IV

A Current in the Earth   127

V

Rescue   175

I

There was a man in the land of Uz . . .
Job 1:1

Help

I saw a girl standing by the railing, looking down at the water where floating things knocked against the slimy rocks. I almost didn't see her. Her head was bent way down toward the water, so that she seemed to be nothing but a coat hanging on a railing, a coat with legs and bare feet. What a wind was blowing that day! It tore the leaves off the tops of the trees and spun them around on the pavement. Men with black hands used steel rods to lift steel plates out of the street. I was in a big hurry. I hadn't a moment to lose, but her feet stopped me. How cold, I thought, with the wind and the splashing water. And there were bits of glass mixed with cinders where she was standing on tiptoe. The lives some people lead, I thought. Then her head rose like a brown moon over her shoulders and her bare feet reversed on the sparkling cinders and she was looking right at me. That was when I nearly had heart failure. You know how it is when you're caught staring at someone, especially in a certain way. I mean I did find her feet attractive, I have to say that. The cold made them shiny and pink, and the cinders had covered them over with gray. The bottoms of her heels were black. I could tell because she'd lifted them so that she could bend her head down over the railing and look at the floating things.

I don't mean to say that her feet were beautiful, but there was something about their pinkness and their dirtiness and the way they were half in the air that put a certain dream into my head, a dream about the way she looked and the kind of person she was. And when she turned around I saw that my dream was true. That was what nearly gave me heart failure. And each thing she did after that gave me another dream and made the dream that came before it come true. It's like when you go someplace and you feel like you've been there before, but you haven't. Then somebody says something you almost knew they were going to say, but you didn't. Then you look out the window in a certain way and you think that you did that before too. Imagine that keeps on happening and happening until it's like you're falling out of the real world and your whole life has become a dream. That's what happened to me. The more I looked at her, the more dreams she put in my head and the more true they became. The first thing was her face. It was just the way I thought it would be when I looked at her feet. Big eyes and a mouth that hangs open a little. She looked like one of those kids that grew up too fast. Like a house with all its windows broken. Like every time she'd touched her mother or her father or anybody, they'd turned around and hit her in the face. But she was beautiful, like one of those winter days when the trees have no leaves on them and they just stand there sticking up at the gray clouds and everything is so still and quiet and cold that it just takes your breath away with its beauty, before it makes you depressed.

She looked right at me and moved her purple lips. I couldn't hear what she said and, though I meant to keep walking, I took a step toward her because her lips put a dream in my head. And then, as I came closer, she opened her coat a little and I saw a line of pinkish white, from her knees to her throat. Can she be naked? I asked myself. My dream answered and the next second I saw that it was true. I wanted to see if the men with the steel bars were looking, but I couldn't turn away. Soon her coat had left her shoulders, flapped in the wind, dropped and hung over the railing, just the way I thought it was when I first saw her. The hand that let go of the coat came down slowly, like a snowflake. She had gooseflesh all over her body, but otherwise didn't seem to notice the freezing wind. Her hair flapped around her head like electricity. "What are you doing?"

I said. "You're gonna freeze to death!" She raised her eyes to heaven like what I'd said was the stupidest thing she'd ever heard. Then her purple lips moved, but I didn't hear what words came out.

All of this I've described took maybe three seconds; a glance, a footstep, and the coat flying from her shoulders. But I felt like I'd known her for years, like she was my daughter, or my best friend's wife. My heart sank just like it would for them. Then in the next second she was clambering up the cold steel bars. "What are you doing?" I shouted. Her feet molded to the bars and she started to walk away from me, so gracefully she must have been a ballerina. "Hey!" I shouted to the men in the street. "Hey!" I don't know what I wanted them to do. I didn't think I could do anything. I'm no hero. But they were crouching to lift up a huge piece of metal and didn't hear me, or didn't pay attention. When I looked back to the railing there was nothing moving across it but the wind. Oh my God! I thought. I was just going about my business and now look what's happened! I ran to the rail and there she was in the water, a little past the floating things. Her body was light green under the water and white when parts of it came out. I ran to the men. "She fell in! Hurry! A girl fell in the water! She's drowning!" "What?" said one of the men. They all followed me to the railing. "Where?" She was gone, nothing but the cold green water and the wind. "I don't see anything out there," said one of the men, "except garbage and somebody's briefcase." It was my briefcase, going up and down on the jagged waves. All my samples and orders, lost! I must have dropped it when I ran to the rail. "Didn't you see her? She was standing here in a coat." (The coat was gone too.) "Then she took it off and she was naked and then she climbed up on this rail. I don't know whether she fell in or jumped." "She's naked?" said one of the workmen, looking at the other two. "Where is she?" They all leaned over the railing and looked at the water. Then the tall one said, "There's no one there."

They say that heroes are not born but made by the moment. Well, that moment made me a hero. I was up on the railing and I leaped into the air. The water was so cold that I felt like I'd crashed face first onto solid ice. I figured she'd sunk under the water, so I tried to dive down, but I was wearing my suit and my overcoat and they both had so much air in them that all my wriggling and kicking couldn't get me more than six inches down. When I came up for air I found that I couldn't breathe. The cold had paralyzed my lungs. I felt like electricity was drilling into every part of me. I remembered that people who fall into the North Atlantic die within three minutes. I opened my mouth as wide as I could, but my throat seemed to have shrunk to the size of a hair. I knew I was going to die, but it didn't seem to matter to me. It was like I looked up and noticed it was an hour later than I thought it was—that's how much it meant to me. In fact, I was even a little comforted, because now I knew why I hadn't been able to see the girl; she had been swept off on the strong current that was now rapidly carrying me away from the land. The electricity went away, or I got too numb to feel it. I heard the voices of the workmen behind me, but they were very tiny, like the whispers of toy soldiers. Then I turned around in the water and saw that the men really were the size of toy soldiers, and they were shrinking. All the buildings of this city I have lived in for so many years were shrinking and rushing past me. I didn't care. I felt like I was being carried away on a smooth silent train. I turned around again to look out ahead over the pale green tops of the waves. I wondered if I could catch up with the girl. I think maybe I saw her, just a few yards ahead of me, in the valley of a wave. I wanted to hold her in my arms.

The Afterlife of Lytton Swain

1. NOWHERE IN SIGHT

After a while the Reverend Lytton Swain, former professor of Religion and Ethics at one of our great Christian universities, grew used to the fact that he was dead. Not that he came to like it; he simply didn't dislike it. That was death: not much caring one way or the other. To whatever degree he did care, he came to conclude, it was merely a matter of habit. He had become a creature of pure intellect. The emotive part of him had dried out, become transparent, crumbly, like the abandoned carapace of a maturing insect.

One day after he had been dead about a month (yes, there was time after death, days and nights, our time, real time, or so it seemed), he was walking down a country road (Swain continued to inhabit the world he had once lived in, this world, our world. All the material objects remained: houses, pens, forks and chairs, even the trees, flowers and lake slime, everything except living people and animals. The countryside of death was inhabited only by the dead, and they were considerably less numerous than Swain would have thought, than simple mathematics would have dictated. Why? Whatever happened to the untold generations of dead that should have been crowding the earth? Swain couldn't figure it. God remained as mysterious and remote in death as in life) when he noticed a thin man in jeans and a ragged army jacket walking toward him. The man's shoes were glossy with flesh-colored mud and his pants' legs were splotchy with it. He was walking in the rut, tromping indifferently through the inches of mud and the ankle-deep puddles. Swain had often noticed this sort of sloppiness among the dead. He was himself walking on the raised, grassy, and comparatively dry center of the road, not because he cared about keeping his feet clean (they were bare), only because Swain in life, though not a finicky man, had never made a mess of himself when he could avoid it, and the habit had not yet died in him.

Swain and the man were approaching one another along a road that divided two cotton fields. The cotton plants were all reddish-brown stem, no leaves, twisting up out of the black earth like fractured wisps of smoke. A moment before it had been pouring rain. Now the clouds were clustered somberly along the horizon and the sky was so blue and high that it was possible to look through it into the vastness of space. This was the sort of meteorological moment that would have caused the living Swain to stop, fill his lungs, and praise the Lord for His bounty. Now it merely struck him as curious, like a long-forgotten photograph of a once-familiar face—curious, but not in a way that implied curiosity: He noticed the wan splendor that surrounded him only to the degree that he noticed he hadn't noticed it.

Swain had been among the dead long enough to know that there was no point paying any attention to them. They were all lost in their indifference, hanging about like old coats, or drifting aimlessly, clots of emptiness moving across empty space. Countless times, particularly before he knew he was dead, he had gone up to one or another of them to ask for directions, or if he could use a toilet (yes, the bladder still functioned, as did the bowels), only to have them turn away without a word, or with only an indecipherable murmur, or, worst of all, only to have them stare right at the place he occupied without seeing him. Now he was like all the rest. He walked among his fellow severed souls as if they were merely shadows or puffs of wind.

Swain and the man in the army jacket came within inches of one another and, as they did so, Swain felt a tug on his sleeve and heard a voice: "Pardon me."

He stopped and looked down at the man, who was about his height but was standing in the rut. Swain saw that the man's yellow-gray hair had been parted symmetrically by the pouring rain. Swain's own head was protected by a checkered hunting cap.

"Pardon me," the man repeated. "Do you know that we are dead?"

There was no reason for Swain to respond to this question; that is, there were none of the old reasons. He didn't want anything from the man, not friendship, not subordination, not love, not information, not amusement; he didn't even feel a social obligation to answer. These were, however, the first words addressed to him in four weeks, and as such, they evoked an all but extinguished response. The first Swain knew of it was when he felt a tremor in his vocal cords.

"Yes," said Swain.

"I just figured it out. Just a minute ago, as the rain was falling on my head, it occurred to me: I'm dead. Everybody here is dead."

At first Swain said nothing. But then it seemed to him that his silence was another form of death, or at least another stage of his death, and that if he didn't answer there would be no reason for him ever to do anything again. He would just remain where he was standing. The rain and the sun and the stars would come and go and he would remain. Truly dead. Like a rock. He said: "My wife told me."

"What?"

"That I'm dead."

"Oh." The man was quiet for a while. Another cluster of thunderclouds was fast approaching, chasing the first. "Is she here?"

"No. I spoke to her on the telephone. Shortly after I left . . . Died, I mean . . ." (The Reverend Swain met his end the night he left his wife. He was drunk. Only a drunk would slap a checkered hunting cap onto his head and storm barefoot into a rainy night proclaiming that he would never return. And only a drunk would think that his obvious impairment was no reason not to drive. A muddy country road. A long skid. A flaming car upside down in a cotton field. By the time the sun rose Swain had been wandering the countryside of death for two hours. He didn't know what had happened to his car and he didn't know why his clothes were such a mess. Sadly, this was not an unfamiliar experience for the Reverend Swain, who, for many years before he died, had had a pronounced tendency to drink more than was wise. Repentant, he went to a diner and called his wife: "I'm sorry, my love, will you please take me back?"

"Who *is* this?"

"I know what you must be thinking . . ."

"Please . . . Not now . . . Who . . ."

"My little sugar precious, I'm so sorry."

There was a long silence and then a low whisper: "Lytton?"

"Yes, my love."

"It *is* you!"

"Of course it is! You didn't think I meant any of those things I said!"

"Oh my Lord! Forgive me, my gracious Lord!"

"There, there now, pet. You didn't do anything. I'm the one who lost his head."

"I can't believe this is happening!"

Swain was a bit puzzled by his wife's behavior. They had, after all, had many such morning-after conversations during their thirty-four years of marriage. "Will you forgive me, my beloved? I'll understand if you have finally sealed your heart to me, but I'm so terribly lonely. Please let me come home."

"But, Lytton . . . Oh my Lord!" A long silence. "You're *dead.*"

"But, my love . . ." Swain made a small noise of mirth. "It can't be as bad as all that."

"No, I mean *dead!* . . . You're dead. I mean *really* dead!"

Swain said: "I was very upset when she told me."

"You weren't really upset."

"I was. I really was."

"Well then, perhaps you weren't really dead yet."

"Perhaps not." Swain no longer quite remembered.

"Look." The man put his left index finger into his mouth. When he drew his hand away the finger was gone. Blood was running down his chin. Blood was making bruise-colored speckles in the mud. He spat his severed finger over the fence into the cotton field. "You see." He held up his bleeding hand. "That is death."

Swain didn't respond.

"You do it," said the man.

Swain still didn't respond. He thought it strange that a dead man should bleed.

"It's easy." The man picked up Swain's hand and drew it toward his bloody mouth.

Swain felt the warmth inside the man's mouth and then the pain. He knew it was pain. He felt it curling up inside his forearm, like fire, setting off subsidiary blazes in his elbow, under his shoulder muscle, and in his cheek just below his eye. But the pain didn't bother him. It was the same feeling, but it had lost its capacity to move him—except perhaps that it made him confused, although his confusion may just as well have been caused by loss of blood.

The man was gone. Nowhere in sight. It was pouring rain. Swain experienced additional flares of pain as he clambered over the rail fence into the cotton field. He remembered the man spitting out his finger just as he had his own. After a long search Swain discovered a finger, lying on a little hill of clotted earth surrounding the base of one of the cotton plants. Swain thought it was his finger. He held it up to his stump and compared it to his other fingers, to the index finger on his other hand. It seemed right, but perhaps it was a little long. Swain searched some more among the cotton plants and in the tall grass that grew up on either side of the fence. Finally he gave up, tucked the finger into his pocket and walked on, in the rut this time, not even noticing the mud that covered his feet and splashed his trouser legs.

It was a strange and paradoxical fact about life after death that, although Swain seemed to exist in time, real time, our time, and in space, real space, our space, nothing ever really happened. There were no effects or causes. For Swain every moment was complete unto itself, entirely separate from every other moment. Every moment was a new beginning. And so he knew perfect freedom, although he didn't really know he knew it. And so, one moment his finger had been bitten off, and then a little later he was in a diner, reaching for a cup of coffee, and there was his finger, intact, slipping into the little loop and lifting the steaming cup to his lips. There may also have been a finger in his pocket, but he never bothered to look.

As he sipped his coffee, the Reverend Swain had a revelation: After sixty-six years of vain struggle to escape the urgings of his piggish flesh, he was finally free. He had at last achieved the capacity for perfect virtue. Desire was a thing of the past, and so, apparently, was pain. Put a bed of hot coals in front of him and he could go to sleep on it. Tempt him with buckets of bourbon, a palace of virgin flesh, world domination, and he wouldn't even sigh. He had been walking around in this divine state (was he an angel?) for at least a month without even noticing. And what is more, now that he had noticed, he hardly cared. That's death for you. This is not to say that a mind long disciplined by the habits of academe and the pulpit could meet the sudden resolution of one of life's chief dilemmas with complete equanimity. He was, in fact, more than a bit troubled by his transcendence, though he wasn't quite sure why. Perhaps it was the fact that it had been accomplished so easily. Anyone could do it, merely by dying. That certainly took away from it. But the longer he thought about it, the more it seemed to him that even had he achieved this elevated state in life, he still wouldn't have found it perfectly satisfying. Being good ought to feel good, and Swain didn't feel much of anything. That was the problem. Merely obeying the Lord's commandments out of duty was too abstract—no, it was worse: A man who refrained from killing only because the Lord had forbidden it and not because he abhorred violence or felt kinship with his fellow man was a moral monster, a Nazi. And wasn't that just what Swain had become?

Swain wasn't sure how to answer this question.

His indecision manifested itself in a long moment of paralysis (he held his cup motionless an inch from his lips) that lasted until it occurred to him that in his present state he had transcended even the Lord's commandments, that only the living could kill, covet, love their enemies, or have lust in their hearts. And then his head began to reel, his cup dropped onto its saucer, and he became more confused than he had been the moment he lost his finger.

2. NOTHING FOLLOWS ANYTHING

Yes, there were inconsistencies after death: Swain's index finger, for example, remained insubstantial, coming and going unpredictably. Equally unpredictable was midnight, which would often intrude with all its impenetrable blackness into the middle of a sunny afternoon. (The reverse would also occur, though not quite so frequently.) And then there were those steaming cups of coffee that kept appearing in diners when there was not even a waitress or a harried cook to serve them. It was a very long time after his death—several months at least; or maybe years?—before Swain began to notice these inconsistencies. And when he did, he generally assumed that they were due to the wandering of his attention; he had, after all, grown rather used to the constancy of the physical world during his long lifetime. It was only after the succession of countless—years, let us say—that he began to suspect it was not his mind but reality itself that was wandering.

In all of his traveling (for Swain himself wandered, barefoot, in his checkered hunting cap, up and down the American continent and even abroad to Europe, Asia, and Africa), he was only able to discuss his suspicion of the world's instability with one other person, Alexander Graham Bell, the inventor. Swain came upon Bell one afternoon of extraordinary clarity and brightness while strolling along the rocky shore of a vast saltwater lake somewhere north, in Maine perhaps, or maybe Canada. He rounded a bend and saw a long, red, cigar-shaped craft rocking gently on the choppy water. Beside the craft, up to his stout middle in the water, was the gray-haired, bearded inventor, banging at something with a wrench and muttering angrily. As Swain was about to walk past, Bell shouted out to him, "Hallo, can you give me a hand?" Swain might never have responded to Bell's entreaty had he not, at that precise instant, tripped and fallen into the freezing water. He rose with his back to the shore and simply forged ahead. By the time Swain was able to steady himself against the canvas hull of the craft, he had stumbled two more times, his hair was streaming with brine, and his checkered cap was lost forever.

"Thanks awfully," said Bell, who was clutching the wrench in one hand and a large nut in the other. "Could you do me the favor of pressing this stanchion down over that bolt there? The thing's a bit stiff and I just can't hold it in place and put on the nut at the same time."

Swain grabbed hold of a red-painted metal bar jutting up out of the green depths and pushed it down until a hole in its flattened end slipped over the indicated bolt. Bell spun on the nut and tightened it with his wrench. "Excellent! At last she's seaworthy again. I might never have gotten that on by myself. . . . You can let go now, by the way."

Swain released the bar, which he had been gripping with both hands.

The great inventor introduced himself and hardly seemed to notice when Swain failed to reciprocate. Bell patted the resonant hull of his strange craft: "My beautiful *Swan!* Have you heard of her?"

"No," answered Swain.

"Don't worry. Hardly anyone has." Bell began to climb a series of indented steps onto the back of the Swan. "Hardly anyone knows half the things I've invented. It's because I never publish."

Bell reached down a thick, freckled hand and pulled Swain up beside him. The two men sat in identical wicker seats on either side of the Swan's spine. Bell pushed a black lever and a huge fan, directly behind their heads, began to chop at the air with a hoarse roar that gradually built into a wavering, multi-toned wail. The boat shuddered, churned awkwardly, and then, slowly picking up speed, began to rise into the air. Soon it was rocketing across the surface of the lake on four thin skis. Spray shot against Swain's face like gravel. The sharp northern air stung his nostrils and earlobes. As the boat devoured the vast distances of the lake, Swain had the strange sensation that the world, this fabulously clear and bright world, had turned to liquid and was rushing over him. "Bet you've never done anything like this before," Bell shouted over the din of wind and motor. In fact Swain had ridden hydrofoils several times, in Florida before his death and in Europe after it. But he said nothing. He was lost in thought.

Bell behaved like no other dead person Swain had ever met. Did the man even know he was dead? Swain asked himself. For a while he wondered if Bell was in fact dead at all. And, briefly, intermittently, Swain speculated that he himself might not be dead. In the presence of this robust inventor it was just conceivable to Swain that he might even have been mistaken about so monumental and all-pervasive a fact.

They were climbing a stony path up from the lake. Bell was enumerating all of the inventions for which he had never gotten proper acclaim: ". . . the audiometer, the photophone, the induction balance, and of course the phonograph record! Tom Edison gets all the praise for that, but the first one was made at *my* laboratory in Washington, D.C. And the aeroplane! That was mine too. I'm talking about the principle, of course. I can't deny that the Wrights got all the pieces together first, but I'd worked out the principle when they were still selling bicycles in Dayton . . ." Swain had known some of this already. He had, in fact, been obsessed by the great inventor's biography in elementary school. At the time it had seemed tremendously significant to him that he had been born the very year Bell had died—and perhaps, after all, it was. ". . . and tetrahedral construction. You've probably noticed that it's caught on everywhere, but do you think anyone associates it with Alec Bell? Not at all, I'm afraid. Damn frustrating is what it is. And it's not been any better since I died. I've invented a machine that can transport visual images over telephone wires. If you wanted to see someone in London, or in Baghdad for that matter, you would only have to call them on the telephone, turn on this machine, and . . ."

"Television," said Swain.

Bell winced and lowered his hand heavily onto Swain's shoulder. "Don't say that word! I know. It's already been invented. Other people have told me about it. Sometimes, at night, I see a strange blue glow . . . *But I did it first!*" The heavy hand came down again. "Damn frustrating! It's as if I hadn't done it at all. I couldn't publish now, even if I wanted to, even if I did have time to write up my results . . ."

"I know what you mean," said Swain. "I too have made discoveries since . . . I mean all this . . ." He gestured at the wide shining lake, the somber blue of the pines, the hill-top fields as luminously green as wet moss. "Sometimes I think—"

"I could give man flight!" said the inventor. "Do you

understand? I've figured it out! I've done it. I don't just mean in an aeroplane. Real flight! With his own wings! Like the gulls." The heavy hand closed on Swain's shoulder, clutching at the bone. "It kills me! It rips me up inside! This being nothing. Do you see? Do you see the tears running down my cheeks?"

Swain saw nothing of the kind. He saw sun-mottled skin, creased, dented, dry as stone. He saw stiff, gray wires of beard twisting together, reaching out into the air but holding within their midst a deep fragrant oil of darkness. He saw darkness again in the two glassy eyes that were not like eyes at all, but holes in a skull, a skull that was not a container but an opening into an emptiness bigger than the world.

"This is my wife," said Bell.

A slender woman, with long, graying hair gathered up behind her head, stood on the polished oak floorboards of the Bell mansion.

"Pleased to meet you," said Swain, who remembered as he spoke that Bell's wife was deaf.

She took his extended hand and said, "Good evening, Mr. Swain. You're just in time for dinner. Won't you please join us?"

Swain looked inquiringly at her husband, who smiled and flicked his own ear. "I know. It's remarkable, isn't it? After all this time she's had a remission. But who knows how long it will last."

Swain followed the Bells into their dining room. The table had already been set for three, and plates of food were already steaming in the light of enormous candles. The heads of numerous animals looked down out of the cluttered Victorian darkness on the edges of the candle-glow. All through the meal Bell talked about how his Swan would help the war effort. He was referring, Swain eventually realized, to World War I. Clearly the man was only imperfectly aware of his death. Mabel Bell watched her husband with the vacant tranquillity of the animals on the wall. Swain never saw her eat, but the food slowly disappeared from her plate. Sometimes she herself disappeared, apparently to have a word with the servants in the kitchen.

At one point Swain looked over to discover his own wife

sitting directly across from him in Mrs. Bell's seat. She was much older than he remembered her being, and perhaps a little taller, but there was no mistake about it: She was wearing her emerald-green evening dress, her favorite, and her eyes glinted with that frantic cordiality that had always so annoyed him. This discovery was so unexpected that Swain was stirred into something quite like astonishment. "Loretta! What are you doing here?"

Two familiar wrinkles formed between her eyebrows. "Hush, Lytton! Mr. Bell is speaking."

"But, Loretta . . ."

She uttered a dismissive "humph" and turned her face away from him, focusing all of her attention on their illustrious host.

"Loretta, please . . ."

"Well, if you must know . . ." She turned back to him. "I'm dead, just the same as you are. Now hush up and eat your greens. They're getting cold."

Swain looked down at his plate. It was empty. When he looked up again, it was into the tranquil gaze of Mrs. Bell.

After dinner the group retired to the sitting room for brandy and cigars. Once more Swain found himself seated beside his wife. They were sharing a small couch. She was holding his hand. But when he spoke to her, she didn't answer. She never met his eye. He was apologizing for the forty years of deception and cruelty to which he had subjected her. It was a speech that had long been in him, since years before his death actually, although his present circumstances gave it a certain poignant twist. He concluded: "And now I come to you, a pure soul, filled with shame, and ask you to forgive me as I am, as I am in essence: not the man who was too weak to resist temptation, but as the man who always meant to do better . . ."

When his words had been absorbed by the silence of the room, Loretta looked at him coldly. "Of course you know it's much too late for that sort of thing, Lytton."

"I know," he answered with a bowed head. "I just . . ." But he didn't continue. He didn't even know what he had intended to say.

"Besides, I'm not the one you should be apologizing to. I got involved with you with my eyes open. I knew all along—or at least I should have—what a piece of slime you were. But poor Marilyn had no choice in the matter . . ."

Swain had never suspected that his wife knew about Marilyn. (Marilyn. Loretta's niece, and Swain's. One hot summer. Fifteen years old. The drooping bikini bottoms. The long walk over the dunes. The avuncular caress. Oh, the piggishness of flesh!)

"But it's even too late to apologize to her," Loretta added.

"Is she dead too?"

Loretta threw his hand disgustedly into his lap. "Of course she is, Lytton. Where have you been! The whole world has ended!"

Swain was about to ask Loretta what she meant by this last remark, when Bell tapped him on the shoulder and whispered conspiratorily, "I want to show you something in our glorious night sky."

As they stepped from the porch and left the glow of the house behind them, Swain found it hard to imagine what sort of glory Bell saw in this starless, moonless sky. The blackness overhead was only surpassed by the blackness of the earth, in which Swain's hands were drifting charcoal smudges and his feet were obscured totally. Bell strode over the invisible fields as if he were on a paved road, while Swain tumbled into every pothole and tripped over every rock. Only when they had descended to the pebbled beach was Swain able to stride shoulder to shoulder with the robust inventor. And it was as the two men thus proceeded beside the dim hissing line of the lake surf, that the Reverend Swain broached the topic that had so recently become an object of his contemplation. "Have you ever noticed," he asked, "that lately . . . that is, since you . . . I mean we . . . that is, have you ever noticed that things are not always consistent?"

"I don't follow you."

"I mean . . . for example, your wife. I was watching her at dinner. She never touched her food, but at the end of the meal her plate was empty."

"Ah, yes. Well, Mabel's always eaten like a bird. Don't let that worry you."

"But her plate was empty. That's what I mean. She didn't eat a thing, but her plate was empty."

"That's the thing about Mabel. She's got a healthy enough appetite, but she always takes such devilishly small bites. It drove me quite round the twist when we were first married. I always had to wait for her to be done, you see."

"But she didn't eat a thing. I watched her. She didn't take a bite of her food, not even a small one."

"I thought you said her plate was empty?"

"It was. That's just what I'm talking about."

"I'm afraid I still don't follow you."

"I'm talking about inconsistencies. Nothing follows anything the way it used to. There are all these effects and not nearly enough causes. Haven't you noticed?" Bell answered only with silence. Swain couldn't see his face well enough to know whether he had even heard the question. After a moment Swain said, "Take my wife for example . . ."

"Lovely woman . . . Bit on the skinny side herself, mind you."

"No. I mean, what is she doing here?"

The inventor's laughter boomed out over the wet stones and riffling lake. "I can't help you with that one, I'm afraid!"

Swain gave up. It wasn't really like him—at least not anymore—to be so insistent. But things had been different since meeting Bell. The man was such a paradox. He made distinctions between the living and the dead seem practically pointless. Swain wondered if he shouldn't try to be more like Bell. He wondered if the inventor hadn't cottoned onto some great secret. But he said nothing. They walked in silence, amid the hissing of the surf and the crunch of their footsteps. As they rounded a bend, a firm, cool breeze began to stir their hair and clothing.

"If you're worried about inconsistency," said Bell, patting him roughly on the back, "take comfort in this—the wind, the laws of aerodynamics." Ahead Swain saw five glowing objects hanging in the air about a hundred yards above the surface of the lake. "My kites," said Bell. "Beautiful, aren't they? Tetra-hedral construction. They're as light as feathers, and almost as strong—proportionally speaking, of course."

The two men proceeded down the shore, and Swain saw that the floating objects were really something closer to aerial sculp-tures than kites. The nearest one was a crescent moon, complete with profiled nose, mouth, and eye. The next down was a cow; the next, a star; and the one after that was a violin. The farthest of the kites was too far away to make out, but it might have been a cat or a dog. Swain asked: "How do they glow?"

"Candles. There's an ordinary candle wired into the center of each kite. The paper walls keep them from being blown out by the wind."

By now Swain and Bell had reached the place where the string of the first kite was tied to a thick stake jutting landwards out of the pebbles. Swain could see the next stake about fifty yards ahead, but the beach was too dark to see farther. He still couldn't make out the exact shape of the fifth kite.

"The wind," repeated Bell. "That's the ticket. The laws of aerodynamics. These kites are kept aloft by a precise balance between their weight, their surface area, the tension of this cord, and the force and direction of the wind. If the relations between things were as unstable as you seem to think they are, none of these kites could stay aloft, none of this"—he swept his arm in a broad arc—"would be here, nor, for that matter, would man"—a large grin expanded under his beard—"be able to fly."

"What do you mean?" asked Swain.

"It's what I was telling you before . . ." Bell looped a piece of string around the top button of Swain's shirt, then drew the string down and tucked it under Swain's belt. "The gift of flight. This is what I could give to mankind, if only . . ." Pulling the string out from under the belt, he took one step back, and then another. He repeated: "If only . . ." Swain was already beginning to feel buoyant. "Hold out your hands," said Bell. "Straight out from your shoulders. That's it. Not so stiff. Just relax. It's really quite easy."

It seemed to Swain as if Bell was shrinking, but after a moment he realized that he himself had been borne aloft by the wind. Bell was now some distance below, gingerly letting out string and shouting, but Swain was already too high to hear. His trousers and shirtsleeves were snapping in the brisk wind. His toes were wiggling in the empty air. The great man of science and the shoreline itself swayed from side to side and grew ever smaller.

Up and up.

Swain had already risen above the level of the other kites.

The fifth one, he could now see, was a rooster, its head tilted back and its beak split by a silent crow. Bell had vanished from sight, sucked into the blackness on the other side of his glowing creations.

Up and up and up.

Now the other kites, all that Swain could see of the world, were only five yellow dots. As he watched, they blinked out all at once, then flickered individually back into sight. A moment later they were raked by blackness once again and vanished for good, consumed by the lowest layer of clouds. For a long while Swain saw nothing. Then a great flank of gray emerged from the blackness and yellowed as it drew near him. Swain continued to rise and passed over the cloud. As he did, he watched a small, wobbling circle of brilliance follow him across its gaseous surface. Overhead he saw a similar glow, skimming the underside of another cloud. The glow grew more and more brilliant as he rose toward it. When finally the cloud enveloped him, he was also enveloped by the glow: steady, pleasant, equally brilliant on all sides of him, fleshly yellow-orange.

The cloud, which had seemed so soft as he approached, was a nest of turbulence. Sharp drops of moisture struck his cheek, stiff winds buffeted him, twisting him on his string, until finally he hadn't the faintest idea whether his feet were facing the earth, the heavens, or the horizon. His string brushed lightly over his face and then wrapped loosely around one leg. It had broken, or Bell had let it go. Swain didn't much care one way or the other. He was not afraid of falling, not so much because he had lost the capacity to fear as because he no longer believed he would fall—or rather, because he no longer believed in the earth.

He knew now that the world he had existed in since his death had not been a world at all, that day had followed night, that rain had alternated with sun, not according to any laws of nature, but because these were the only terms in which he could conceive of his existence. And these terms, he also knew, had been obsolete since the moment his car overturned and burst into flame. It was only a matter of time, which had itself become obsolete, before these terms were degraded by their own inapplicability and he would become the isolate "I" in Descartes's *cogito*. Once upon a time Descartes's formulation had seemed irrefutable to him, a matter of common sense, the rock of fact on which he built the palace of his faith. Now it was as mysterious and insubstantial as the illuminated vapor through which he was drifting. Without the world to think about, could the "I" of him even be said to be thinking? And if it was not thinking, then what would it be? But even these questions hardly mattered to the Reverend Swain. That's death for you: the perfect illumination that is indistinguishable from darkness.

3. NO TIME LEFT

Let's call it a room. And in the room there are men in white gowns with knives.

"What happens now?" asked the Reverend Swain.

"We prepare you," said one of the men.

"For what?"

"For what happens next."

Swain felt a slight tug and looked down to find his intestines dangling out of his belly like wet laundry out of a washer.

"Don't worry about that," said the man standing in front of him.

"I'm not," said Swain. He was, however, finding it hard to remain on his feet. Something in his head was zinging in circles like a ball-bearing in a steel bowl. When he reached to support himself on the shoulders of one of the men, he was surprised to discover he was missing a hand. Several of the men came together and lowered him gently to the floor.

"Where am I going?" asked Swain.

"Where do you think?" said the man kneeling beside him.

Swain laughed. "I don't like to think about it." He felt something happening to his left leg. "Don't you know?"

"That's not our business," said the kneeling man.

"We're not the ones who decide," said somebody else.

The work was hard but the men were well-practiced. Swift slices. A few quick chops. A quivering. A sudden dullness in the eyes. It was all over in a matter of minutes.

"Poor sucker," said one.

"Cooperative though," said another.

The men didn't particularly like their work. It was called "paring away," but none of them really believed that there was anything left when they were done. They felt guilty. They felt as if they were playing dirty tricks on their trusting subjects. And they were made fun of for this by their employers, who called them "boneheads," "bowelsuckers," "bloodyboys," and who casually dismissed them as having "an insufficiently developed capacity for abstraction." But their employers never got their hands dirty. They never saw the mess on the floor, or suffered that moment of weary silence at the very end, after the last hiss of steel. The men trusted the evidence of their own eyes. They trusted common sense. They trusted simplicity. But nothing could stop their employers from laughing. It was an age-old conflict really. One of the oldest.

Nobody

~~~~~~

"Don't you think we ought to at least take a look?" she said, slipping a map out of her hip pocket.

"Forget it," he said. "I remember now. We didn't get there by a trail. We just hiked into the woods." He had only been to the lake once, ten years earlier, but was sure he would find it. The landscape was exactly as he remembered it: the long valley like a green blanket folded between two legs, the twin peaks, directly opposite one another, like a pair of knees. He was certain that if he drew a line between the peaks and followed it east into the next valley, it would lead him straight to the lake. "Besides," he said, "the lake won't be on the map. It's not really a part of the park. That's why no one ever goes there." He smiled. "That's why we'll be all alone."

Shaking her head, she put the map away and followed him off the trail and up the gentle slope under the pine trees.

It hardly mattered at first that there was no trail. Hiking over a copper-colored mattress of pine needles under the low darkness of the branches was like walking through a room. But it was hot, even in the perpetual shade: There was no breeze, the air was steamy, and they were both carrying heavy packs. As the slope got steeper the trees became stunted and thin. The sun shot through the scanty foliage to form bright, burning globs on the tufty grass and lichen-covered stones. The heat of the baking mountainside and of their own sweaty bodies rose to press their cheeks like hot silk.

He took off his shirt. A little while later she took off hers: Why not? They hadn't seen another person for more than an hour, and if all went as planned they wouldn't see anyone for days. The small coolness of the sweat evaporating off her breasts made her happy. She reached out to take his hand. "This is wonderful," she said. "I'm so glad we're doing this."

He stopped and took her in his arms, her breasts compressing against the hot slipperiness of his ribs. "So am I," he said.

They ate lunch in the shade of a solitary boulder on the granite hump of the easternmost "knee," looking across the whole of the valley out of which they had climbed. Beyond the opposite peak they could see other mountains rippling like fuzzy green wavelets into the yellowish summer haze.

Carefully repacking their used plastic wrap and juice bottles, they crossed over the bulging granite to its eastern side. The trees grew too thickly for them to see where they were headed, so he simply set off along the imaginary line from the opposing mountain and she followed. The land dropped steeply for a few hundred yards, but then leveled off into a barely perceptible decline—which confused him. He remembered this half of the hike as a long, difficult descent between overgrown boulders and tall pines. Instead they were making easy progress through knee-high grass under the sparse coverage of twisted, mossy scrub trees. Only when they had been traversing this pleasant terrain for close to an hour did he venture, "I think we might not be going in the right direction."

"Why?"

"We should be going down a steep slope."

"We are going down a slope. Maybe you just exaggerated it in your memory."

"No. I remember, it was practically vertical."

She swayed her head in annoyance. They had been hiking for close to four hours now and she was getting tired. "So, what do you think we should do? I can't take this heat much longer."

He thought that they should return to the peak and try to get a clear view, maybe by climbing a tree, but he said, "Let's just keep going and see what happens."

"No. Let's look at the map." She slipped the map out of her pocket. It was damp with sweat and the pages had to be pried apart.

"See, I told you," he said. "This map is no good." He jabbed at a blank spot in the upper-left-hand corner. "This is where we are. We left the park when we went over the top of the mountain."

"Okay, but that's not the point." She snapped the two halves of the limp map together. "I just don't want to keep walking and walking, unless we're going to get somewhere."

"We're going downhill," he said. "That's the main thing."

While she struggled to get the map back into her pocket, he strode ahead and she had to run to catch up with him. For a time they walked side by side without talking or even looking at one another. But then the land began to decline more steeply and the scrub trees yielded to maples and oaks. "Ah, this is more familiar," he said, and took hold of her hand. She said nothing, but returned the gentle squeeze he gave her fingers.

Soon they came to a small clearing. He pointed at the ground and said, "Blueberries."

"What?"

"Blueberries. All around us. These are blueberries."

"Are they ripe?"

"I don't know. Taste one."

She crouched. "Are you sure they're blueberries?"

"Positive. They grow all over these woods."

She reached out and plucked, lifting a tiny black globe to her lips, first sniffing it, then giving it a tentative nibble. At a small burst of sweetness she pushed the remainder of the berry into her mouth and looked up at him, smiling. "They're delicious."

"I told you."

She plucked two berries at once and popped them into her mouth. "That's it! This is as far as I go! I hereby declare this a rest stop."

"But the lake's probably just ahead. Look, there's a steep drop right over there. It probably goes straight down to the lake."

"I don't care. I can't go another step without some sustenance." She let herself be drawn backward by her pack, dropping heavily onto her buttocks. "You go on if you want. I'm going to gorge on blueberries." She slipped her arms out of her pack and it rocked backward into the shrubs behind her.

He hesitated a moment, then turned and lumbered resolutely toward the edge of the bluff. She heard him call out something before he dropped out of sight, but he wasn't looking at her so she couldn't understand it.

She took a swig from the plastic-tainted water in her canteen. Pouring a little into the palm of her hand, she splashed it onto her burning shoulders, then leaned forward with her arms stretched over her head until the stiff spades of tiny blueberry leaves tickled her brow. Directly in front of her mouth she noticed a plump berry, sticking up above the rest. With a small grunt, she dropped the extra inch and lipped the berry into her mouth. She sat up and began to eat in earnest, plucking berries with each hand until she couldn't hold any more, cramming whole palmfuls into her mouth. The berries were extremely sweet, almost like jam, but tinged with a watery sourness. Between mouthfuls she exclaimed aloud: "God, these are the best blueberries I've ever had . . . I'll never be able to eat store-bought blueberries again . . . Delicious!" Eventually she realized that she was talking to herself, but thought, "Why not? There's no one to hear," and kept it up until her self-consciousness took the fun out of it.

She heard grunts and a trampling of leaves. An orange backpack and a red face rose over the edge of the slope. "So what's the news, Daniel Boone?" she said.

He strode toward her across the grass, panting slightly. "We're here. I was right. The lake's just over the bluff."

"Fantastic." She chomped through another mouthful. All around her lips and down her chin were purple-gray smudges. "Sit down and have some blueberries. They're incredibly delicious."

He eased down beside her and freed himself from his pack with a groan. She held up her latest harvest and he ate them out of her hand.

"This is unbelievable!" she said. "A beautiful lake, all the blueberries we can eat, and no one to share it with but ourselves."

Smiling around his mouthful he reached across and cupped her breast in his hot moist hand. When he had swallowed he leaned across and kissed her, licking the sweetness from her mouth and then tasting the saltiness on her neck.

A while later, barefoot and naked, their bodies speckled with berry pulp, they stepped gingerly down the leafy slope to the lake. He carried two joints and a box of matches cupped in one hand, and placed them carefully in a dry niche of rock before diving into the cold, clear lake.

They swam hard a few yards, feeling clean and strong, then eased into a slow, steady breaststroke, heading for the farthest point they could see. The longer they swam the more convinced he became that this was not the lake he had visited ten years earlier. The trees leaning out over the shimmery surface were maples and beeches, not pines; there were outcroppings of whitish, layercake rock rising five or ten feet above the water, but no granite cliffs; and the lake was almost as broad as it was long, not thin and canal-like. As they got farther out he realized that the lake was even larger than it had first seemed. What he had thought was merely a more thickly wooded portion of the far shore was actually a peninsula concealing—from the color of the water and the way it rippled—perhaps a whole other half of the lake. He said nothing about his doubts, however. This lake was as beautiful as the other. Why not just enjoy it?

When they rounded the peninsula they both stopped swimming as if they'd run into an invisible wall. On a grassy hill, half hidden by two towering hemlocks and an outgrowth of bush, was a small, squarish, brown house. "I don't remember that being there," he said softly. One of the house's neat, white-framed windows was partly open, and there was an aluminum canoe lying bottom-up on the steep grassy slope.

"It looks occupied," she said.

"Oh, well." He shrugged as he treaded water. "Boy," he said, "this place sure has changed." He couldn't meet her eyes. Without a word, he turned and started swimming back to the wide flat rock from which they had dived into the lake.

Lifting himself out of the water, he stretched out on the hot hard surface under the strong sun. The blood rose to his cheeks almost immediately and he could tell that he would be making frequent dives into the water to cool off. She clambered up onto the rock and sat beside him, knees drawn up to her shoulders and arms folded across her shins. She looked at him sideways, giving him a fresh, athletic, but also awkward smile. Feeling a surge of love for her, he sat up, wiped his fingers on the rock, and reached for the joints.

She said: "Don't you think we ought to go back and put something on?"

"Oh, don't worry." He kissed her cool, dripping cheek. "It's just one little house. They can't even see us from there. Besides, who cares? If we can't go skinny-dipping at a mountain lake, where can we?"

She crinkled her lips in a dubious smile, but said nothing. He wanted to make love with her again, but knew this was not the right moment. He handed her a joint, put the other in his mouth, and struck a match.

They talked contentedly while they smoked and then lay back, pillowing their heads on their crossed arms. They talked some more but with increasing intervals between their remarks. Soon they had each fallen into a superficial slumber in which their thoughts dithered incoherently, but they never ceased to be aware of the summery buzzings, the quiet clucking of the water, and the gentle stirring of the warm breezes in their body hair.

He awoke with a start, overheated and dry in the mouth. Woozily, scraping his foot on a blade of rock, he propelled himself away from the shore in a shallow dive, but found that the lingering effects of the marijuana made shooting weightlessly under the surface unpleasantly disorienting. Turning back, he took a gulp of the fishy-tasting water, only partly assuaging his thirst. As he climbed onto the rock she sat up, her face deep red and beaded with sweat.

"You should take a dip," he said, stroking her hot cheek with his cool hand.

She jerked her head back. "No. I want to go up and get our stuff. I don't think we should have left it all this time."

"All right." He was looking forward to a drink from his canteen, and perhaps to opening one of the bottles of wine they had each carried in their packs. It was time to set up camp. He glanced along the lake shore for a good spot to pitch a tent, but couldn't see any. Once he was dressed, he would do a more thorough exploration.

They climbed the slope, digging their fingers and toes into the blackened leaves and loose moist earth. They should have been able to see their belongings as soon as they lifted their heads above the edge of the bluff, but it wasn't until they had nearly reached the clearing that he said, "Wait a second," and simultaneously she exclaimed, "Somebody's taken our stuff!"

Something in him violently rejected the suggestion that their belongings had been stolen. "Paranoid nonsense," he thought as he hurried ahead. But when he reached the center of the clearing and saw no trace of their clothing or packs, not even a sock, he was suddenly certain that someone was watching him. He wanted to drop to his belly to hide.

She was standing beside him. "Maybe this isn't the right spot," she said.

"Of course it is!" he answered angrily. "The grass is all flattened out."

"But you were just walking on it."

"Not here I wasn't."

"Look." She pointed to a bright spot through the trees. "Maybe that's where we were."

He was sure that she was wrong, but followed her anyway, and kept following even when it was obvious that their stuff wasn't in that clearing either. The packs were radiant orange— not easy to miss even in the thickest foliage. They stopped in the middle of the clearing.

"This is it," she said. "I remember looking at that tree."

"No it isn't. It was back there."

"Listen, I was sitting here a lot longer than you were. I remember looking at that tree."

He was furious at her. This was nothing like the place where they had made love. "Look, it doesn't matter where we were. Our clothes aren't in either place."

"Oh, Christ! I can't believe it." She laughed weakly. "No one will believe it when we tell them." Suddenly terribly aware of her nakedness, she grabbed hold of his upper arm with both hands and pulled herself close.

"All right, you fucking bastards!" he shouted. "The joke's over. Ha! Ha! You can keep the wine and the dope, just give us back our clothes." His voice was swallowed instantly by the leaves, the branches, and the chirrupping birds, without the faintest whisper of an echo or reply.

"Don't shout," she said softly, squeezing his arm.

"This is un-fucking-believable." He shook his head mirthlessly.

"Do you think someone really took our stuff?"

"Come on, you assholes!" he shouted again.

"Stop it!" she whispered. "You're scaring me."

He shook his arm free and stepped away. "You'd think that if someone took our things they'd stick around to watch our reaction."

"Oh God, I can't stand it!" she said. "This is really awful, you know that. We don't have our car keys, we don't have our money. I mean, even if we get out of here what are we going to do?" She tried to look as though she still thought this was funny, but her brow was wrinkled anxiously and she'd folded her arms tightly across her breasts, clutching at her sides.

He pried one of her hands loose and squeezed it. "Look, let's go back down to the lake and try again. Maybe we came up at the wrong place."

They retraced their steps down to the rock and could find no sign of their having descended the bluff along any other path. As they climbed back up he found a stout stick that he used to steady himself on the loose soil and then carried in his right hand as a club. They both laughed at the ridiculous sight he made, and cracked caveman jokes, but everything they said was half intended for the skulking observers they imagined behind every tree. After a while she too picked up a stick and walked with it raised threateningly. They made their way in ever widening circles around the two clearings and along the bluff, at first hoping to find a third clearing with their things lying miraculously as they had left them, and then simply trying to find the tree or bush where their things had been abandoned. They found nothing. They scratched themselves on brambles. They injured their feet on hidden rocks and sharp sticks. She walked through a patch of poison ivy and he, in a moment of tenderness and guilt, confessed that he had led her to the wrong lake. She was furious, as if his having gotten them lost was somehow the reason their clothes had been stolen. "We're not lost," he said. "I know exactly how to get back."

Finally they gave up. It was getting late and they were hungry. They sat down in a blueberry patch, had an unsatisfying dinner ("I hate these things," she said), and tried to decide what they were going to do. The sun was getting low in the sky and they would have had no hope of getting back to their car before dark, especially on bare feet. He still had the box of matches, so they could build a campfire, but neither of them relished the idea of huddling naked on the cold ground the whole night through. Finally he said, "Why don't we just swim over to that house again? I mean, it will be sort of weird going up to their door and all, but we'll just have to explain."

Their second crossing of the lake was an ordeal. They were starving and exhausted, not only from their exertions, but from worry. They drank the lake water as they swam and made grim jokes about diarrhea. By the time they came in sight of the house, the sun was down and the mosquitoes were out. In one of the windows there seemed to be a light burning, but it may only have been the reflection of the sky. While he waded ashore she remained squatting up to her neck in the water, partly out of modesty, but mostly to keep off the mosquitoes.

He stole up the slope, crouching like a movie commando. The canoe was tied to a metal stake, completely overgrown by the high grass. As he hurried by, the top of the stake raked his foot and he tumbled forward into the grass, suppressing a howl. A few moments later, he limped up the three steps to the door and knocked tentatively. The window beside the door was dark. He looked around for some sort of concealment, but there was nothing, unless he wanted to rip up a couple of handfuls of grass. He knocked a second time and called out, "Excuse me! Hello! Is anybody home?" Still no answer. He twisted the black metal knob and the door fell open. "Hello," he called into the pitch-black interior, imagining some frightened country couple with a shotgun trained on him. Not a sound came from inside the house, not a creak or a rustle.

Looking over his shoulder, he saw that she was already walking up the hill from the lake, her pale skin luminous in the dusk. He reached his hand inside the door, feeling along the wall for a light switch, but found only a couple of bent nails. Stepping into the darkness, he waved his extended hands, hoping to catch the string of an overhead light, and walked straight into the edge of a table. He heard a soft footstep and saw her silhouette in the door behind him. "It was too creepy just sitting out there alone in the lake," she said.

"I can't find the light."

She started waving her hands in the darkness. "Maybe there's no electricity."

He continued across the room, to where there was another door, and felt along the wall beside it.

"Ah-ha!" she exclaimed, startling him.

"What?"

"A kerosene lantern." She held it in front of the door so that he could see.

"Great. Now all we need are matches."

The matches were on the shelf right next to the lantern. She struck one and in its light saw another lantern beside the other door. They took both lanterns outside so that they could see what they were doing. Soon a lime-yellow glow lit up the fronts of their bodies and made the gray sky turn black.

They each picked up a lantern and went back through the door. The house had only a single room, one side of which was just a simple, rustic kitchen with a wood-burning stove, a zinc sink, and a hand-operated water pump. The other side, however, was furnished like a Victorian study. The walls were covered with varnished shelves, which were tightly stuffed with books, folders, and loose sheaves of paper. Still more books were stacked all across the floor, in tiny pyramids: the largest volumes on the bottom and the smallest on top, with all the corners alined. Even the single bed was half-covered with books, allowing only a two-foot strip for sleeping. Against one wall, crammed under the low ceiling, was a looming mahogany wardrobe, and on the other wall, inside a glass case, was the most astonishing item in the whole place: an ancient painting, done in gold-leaf, bright pinks, blues and grays on a worm-eaten piece of wood, depicting a throned Jesus Christ surrounded by angels, winged lions and winged cows, with a tiny monk kneeling at his feet.

They stood in front of the painting with both lanterns.

"Shit," he said softly.

"It looks like something that should be in a museum. Do you think it's real?"

"Of course it's real."

"Don't touch it."

"I wasn't going to touch it." He drew his hand back from the glass.

"And they don't even keep this place locked up," she said.

"Maybe that's because they just went for a walk."

"No, look. There aren't any locks on the doors."

The clothes in the wardrobe—men's clothes—were huge. When he stepped into a pair of khaki pants and pulled them up to his waist, there was more than enough leg left to cover his foot, and the waist was so wide that when he let go the pants dropped right down to his ankles.

She laughed. "This guy must be a giant!"

"Let's hope he's a friendly giant."

They each put on ballooning white T-shirts that they pulled from neat stacks at the bottom of the wardrobe. She didn't really need to wear anything else, but found a pair of olive shorts with big pockets and a strap-like belt that she could draw tight around her waist. He rolled up his pants legs and used some twine from one of the kitchen cabinets as a belt. They looked at each other and laughed. "You look sort of sexy in these oversized clothes," he said, putting his arm around her.

"You don't." She twisted away. "You look like a little kid."

He swatted her buttocks and went over to the food cabinets.

She sat down at the long table, which was half-covered over with books, picked up the top one—a library book with numbers on the spine—and flipped to the title page: *Revelations of Divine Love* by Mother Julian of Norwich. Putting the volume back on the stack, she asked, "What do you think we should do?"

"I don't know about you, but I'm going to make some dinner." He reached both arms into one of the drawers. "Look, here are some potatoes."

"Hold on a second . . ."

"What?" He put four big potatoes down onto the table.

"I don't know . . ." She shrugged. Looking at the potatoes she realized how hungry she was. "I mean, what if the guy comes back? Here we are in his clothes and . . . you know. I mean, we can't just take the place over."

"When he comes back we'll just have to explain that this was an emergency, all of our things were stolen, we were starving, and so on."

"That's fine as long as he isn't the guy who stole our things."

"Oh, don't be so paranoid."

She wanted to say, "That was a joke, you idiot!" Or "Would you stop being so condescending!" But she was too angry. She thought that if she said a word she would burst into tears. Feeling that she might start to cry anyway, she got up from the table and went over to take another look at the painting. Now that the lights were on the other side of the room, the painted figures were just dim shadows against the faintly luminous gold. She pulled open the glass door but couldn't see any more clearly. "I can't believe this guy doesn't keep this place locked," she said. "He must be some sort of a nut, a recluse."

"Nothing but potatoes and onions." He was looking disgustedly into the drawers. "How're we going to cook these things? If we light up the stove this place will be unbearable."

"He must have something that doesn't have to be cooked." She went over to the cabinet and pulled the plastic top off one of a series of coffee cans. "Raisins," she said. She pulled open another: "Peanuts."

"God, I'm sick of eating like a squirrel."

"Maybe there's a garden."

"That's a good idea. There must be a garden." He picked up his lantern and started for the door. "You keep searching in here and I'll go see what I can find."

She looked through the remaining cupboards and containers, finding a big bag of rice, another of pistachio nuts, a dozen jars of peach preserves, several boxes of crackers, three gallon bottles of Johnny Walker Red, one of them half-empty, and a kerosene stove.

She decided to write the owner of the house a note, explaining why they had been forced to trespass, giving their addresses, and promising to send back his clothes, cleaned and pressed, with a check for the food they had eaten. Even if he came back before they left, the existence of the note would help convince him that they really had not been planning to simply pillage his home and run.

She found a box of pens and a spiral notebook on the table beside the stack of books. Flipping the notebook open, she saw at once, from the dated entries, that it was a diary. Feeling a twinge of embarrassment, she averted her eyes as she turned toward the end of the book to find a blank page. But when she got to an entry made that very day, she could not resist taking a look:

I have come here to be closer to God, but every day and every night my solitude is invaded by the Devil. Is there no escape from the stench of doubt, or from the fire of rage and the ice of despair? Today Your adversary snatched my last and most beautiful sweetness: Your caress, my Lord, Your majestic tenderness that had been able to calm me in the bitterest of my frenzies, the way a mother's caress can calm even the tiniest of infants. Today the last shred of my innocence was taken from me and I was cast adrift in a world of relentless sin.

I was on the lake, in my canoe, with my rod and my line, as I am every morning—and it was just such a morning as I came here for. The sun was rising, there was steam on the water and the only sounds were the calls of the birds and the small splashes of the fish stealing their breakfasts from the still surface. I felt that I could breathe You in, oh Lord. I felt that if there could be such sweetness and joy in the world, then the Lord of Love must reign in Heaven. It was as these wondrous feelings lit up my heart that the Devil murdered me without severing my soul from my body.

Oh Lord, he whispered to me that this joy was nothing more than deception and sensuality! He said, "How can you let your faith in God depend upon a movement of the heart?" He said, "Is this any more proof of the Lord's existence than physical love?" Oh my dear God, when I saw the course his arguments were taking, I wanted to leap into the water and breathe it until my lungs were flooded. Only my shame preserved me. Weak with shame, I pulled myself to shore. Weaker with doubt I sit here now.

The Devil has tortured me with his cruelest weapon, which is Your Own Truth. I know that is why, in Your Infinite Justice, You suffered him to come unto me. If I am to come closer to You, oh Lord, I must learn to live without You. I know that I have sinned to let my faith depend upon anything of this world, even upon the movement of my heart. I know that my faith must be its own inspiration, that it must urge me toward You as fiercely and with as little cause as my living flesh urges me to live—and more so.

I am filled with shame! Shame! My heart is pounding. My brow is dripping, but my fingers are as cold as ice. The Devil is stronger than I am. Even now as I speak to You his arguments are working in my mind, robbing me of conviction, turning my words to hypocrisy. When I say, "I believe," I do not believe what I say. This morning I spoke to You as

a lover and I felt beloved. Now I pray that You are listening
to my prayers, that Your eyes look down on the page as I
write. The Devil tells me that I am writing to nobody, to
nothing. I am weak. I am weakening. I cry out to You for
rescue and know that I shall not be rescued.

The door flew open and she leapt out of her seat.

"Look what I've got!" he said. "Lettuce, fresh basil, and tiny
carrots." He dumped his earth-speckled harvest onto the table
in front of her.

"You scared me," she said angrily. Her heart was pounding
and she actually felt dizzy.

"What's the matter with you?" he asked mockingly.

She turned the diary around so that he could read it. "Look
at this."

As soon as his gaze fell upon the open pages he let out a loud
"Hah!" and read with an amused smirk. She got up from the
table and stood against the wall, out of the glow of the lamps,
with her arms folded.

"So what about it?" he asked, looking up at her with the
same smirk. "The guy's a religious nut."

"I think he's crazy," she said in a low voice.

"So's everybody!"

"Stop talking like that. This is serious. This guy is seven feet
tall and he thinks the Devil is talking to him. I don't want to be
here when he comes back."

"Don't worry about this shit. My grandmother used to talk
just like this. The Devil tempted her four and five times a day.
Seriously. This guy's just some sort of born-again twirp. They
all talk like this. Besides, look at all these books. How could
anybody who reads so much be dangerous!"

"I'm not going to stay here," she said, suddenly furious.
"Let's just pack up some food and go, I've dealt with enough
weirdos for one day."

"Go where? We don't even know where the fuck we are!
Besides, it's pitch black out there. I couldn't see four feet in
front of me, even with the lantern. If I hadn't tripped over the
garden, I never would have found it." He walked around the
table and put his arm across her shoulders. "Oh, come on,
love. What are you so worried about?"

"I don't know," she said in a small voice. "It's been a pretty weird day, in case you hadn't noticed." All at once, surprising even herself, she burst into tears. He sat down on the bench beside the table and drew her into his lap. She let herself be comforted.

They boiled the potatoes on the back steps over the kerosene stove. He found the bottles of Johnny Walker and poured them each a glass, which she drank even though she hated the taste. While they waited for the potatoes to be done they ate the fresh vegetables in a delicious, if dressingless, salad. After the potatoes they finished an open bottle of peach preserves, smearing it on crackers, and consumed a huge heap of pistachio nuts. They hardly talked. She was too tired and he was absorbed by their absent host's diary. He would flip a few pages, crack a nut, and then read while he chewed. She didn't think he should be looking at the diary and got increasingly angry as she watched him, but didn't say anything. Between the Johnny Walker and her exhaustion, she wanted nothing but to put her head down and go to sleep.

After reading one passage with particular interest, he glanced over at her with a mischievous smile and said, "At last I've gotten to the root of the problem!" She just looked at him coldly as if she hadn't heard him. He continued unperturbed. "Actually, this is pretty interesting. This guy must be some kind of millionaire. He's always going on about the curse of riches and how it's easier for a camel to get through the eye of a needle and all that. I think he was born rich. It doesn't look like he's ever had a real job. He talks about his inventions. He was working on some sort of new kind of wing. But I don't know. I think it might all have been a crazy fantasy. I mean, this guy is definitely some kind of a nut. Half the stuff he says in here doesn't make any sense at all. He keeps talking about 'man-angels' flying on 'love-power' and 'levitational solitude.' Anyhow, finally he decided to give it all up. He left his wife and kids, everything, and came out here to lead a life of meditation and atonement, 'to naked follow the naked Christ,' he says, like Saint Francis. But the thing is there was some other reason too. He's always going on about how despicable he is, about his 'dark secret,' about how his wife hates him and how he deserves to be hated after what he did. At first I thought it was just because he left her, but it's something else. He never says what it is though, until at last it all comes out. Listen to this:

'It's no use. I cannot hide from myself, from my fate, not even here in the purity of God's creation. The awful urge came on me again today, out of nowhere. I hadn't been possessed by it in weeks. I thought I was finally free. But no. There's no justice to it, no reason. It's simply there, what I've been given. I hate it! Dave again. I brought the Jeep into the garage even though there was nothing wrong with it. I stood next to him as he looked under the hood. And I kept asking him questions. Such stupid questions! He despises me. He is right to despise me. And he would despise me more if he knew—' "

"Stop it!" She grabbed the book and slammed it shut. "This is private! We can't go snooping into this poor guy's life!"

"What does it matter? We don't even know him."

"How would you like it if somebody went snooping into the privacy of your thoughts? We're this guy's guests. We should be considerate."

"Oh, for Godsakes, don't make such a big deal out of it. If the guy's so private, he should have locks on his doors."

"You make me sick!" She got up from the table and started clearing their dishes. "Suppose he'd come in here while you were reading that?"

"Well, he didn't," he said in a low voice.

She brought the dishes over to the sink and put them down carefully. That was the end of her strength. She couldn't do another thing. She lowered her head onto her arms, which were crossed on the edge of the sink, and didn't move for a long while. Finally she returned to the table, rubbing her face. "What are we going to do?"

"Sleep, I guess."

"We can't sleep here," she said, but wanted nothing more than to walk over to the bed and collapse.

"Look, it must be nearly eleven. If he's not back now, he probably won't be back tonight."

She was too tired to know if this line of reasoning made sense. She merely went over to the bed and started moving the stacks of books onto the floor. He turned down one of the lanterns until it went dark and brought the other one over to her. When the bed was clear she fell across it in all of her clothes.

"Aren't you going to get undressed?" he said, pulling off his shirt. "It's hot."

She didn't answer. By the time he turned off the second light she was asleep.

In the middle of the night she awoke from a bad dream, drenched in sweat. She lay looking up into the perfect blackness, listening to the strange creaks of the house and the rustling in the woods. She wanted to get out of her hot clingy clothing, but for a long while she didn't dare. Finally she decided that she was being ridiculous. The owner clearly wouldn't be coming back this late. Besides, there was always the sheet if she needed to cover herself. She sat up and slipped out of the huge clothes, placing them right next to the bed where she could easily grab them. When she lay back down she realized that he was awake. "It's hot," he said, but she didn't answer. She felt his hands moving over her body and soon she too wanted to make love. When it was over they both fell deeply asleep, still in a wet embrace.

"Holy shit!" he was saying. "Holy shit!" There was a huge white globe glaring in the window just above the bed. He was trying to climb over her and she was trying to climb out from under him. Beams of cold gray light shot across the cabin. There was a deep rumbling outside.

"What's happening?" she said, tumbling onto the floor.

"He's back."

"Has he seen us?"

"I don't know."

They were crouching with their hands on the floor, scuttling monkey-style toward the back door.

"Wait a second, our clothes!" she said.

The light went off. The rumbling stopped. A car door creaked. After a long moment of paralysis they turned and were out the back door, as naked as they had entered it.

"This is stupid," he said when they had nearly reached the water's edge. He grabbed hold of her arm and pulled her back toward him. "What are we running away from?"

"I'm not going back up there," she said.

"But what are we going to do? We haven't got any clothes. We haven't got anything. We need help."

She didn't answer. Up at the house a lime-yellow glow was rising in the windows.

"Let's just stay here a bit and see what happens," he said.

Before she could respond, the back door of the house opened

and they saw the silhouette of the owner standing against the lit interior. There was no place for them to hide, so they froze exactly as they had been standing, his hand still clutching her arm. They couldn't tell if he could see them. There was no moon. It was very dark. He stood at the top of the steps for a long time without moving or speaking, then went back inside and closed the door.

They waited amid some tall reeds for almost half an hour before creeping carefully back up the hill. Taking shelter behind a tree trunk in the deep blackness beside the house, they looked in through an open window and saw a man—heavy-gutted with tufty brown hair—kneeling beside the bed, a handful of books resting on his thighs. At first he seemed to be staring straight at them, but the expression on his face was merely thoughtful. He showed no sign of having seen them. For a long time he remained motionless, then lifted the books and examined their spines. He took one book out of the middle of the pile and put it on top, then placed the pile on the bed. He seemed very tired, as if all he wanted to do was lie down, but he didn't. He picked up another handful, shuffled them into some sort of order, and put them on the bed beside the books he had just set down.

When at last he had finished, he slapped his hands onto his knees and seemed to shut off, become inanimate, with his eyes staring emptily across the room. Then he was moving again, lifting himself slowly to his feet, as if his back hurt. He was indeed very tall. His head nearly touched the ceiling. He had a broad sack of a belly and a heavy, almost Neanderthal brow. His long cheeks had been corrugated by age and exposure. He looked to be in his fifties, but moved as if he were seventy.

He walked over to the table, stopped, flipped open the cover of his diary, closed it again, and picked up the bowl of pistachio nuts and the glasses that had contained their drinks. He said something aloud, but they couldn't make it out. Then he disappeared from view in the direction of the sink, reappearing a moment later and stopping beside the table. Once more he became inanimate, standing as still as a tree in the forest, except for the fingers of one hand, which were drumming lightly on the table. He disappeared in the direction of the back door. They heard the door crack and the resonant scrapes of his feet on the top step, but their view of him was blocked by the corner of the house. After a moment there came the flutter and splat of a stream of urine falling into the grass. A moment of silence, then a sigh and a murmured, "Lord, no."

The door closed. Again he was by the table. The fingertips of his right hand were pressed against the middle of his forehead, as if he were trying to remember something. "Well, there's nothing else . . ." he said in a deep, gentle voice. He lifted a rolled bundle of the clothes they had borrowed and the sheets they had slept on from a bench and stuffed it into a straw hamper underneath the painting. He said something more, but they couldn't understand it. Another moment of extended inactivity. He walked back to the table, and around it, so that he was standing quite close to the window. He turned a full circle, and then again, slowly, examining the room. He lowered himself heavily onto the bench and rested one elbow on the table beside the diary. Once more he lifted the tips of his fingers to the center of his forehead. There was a half-empty juice glass of amber liquid—the Johnny Walker—on the table in front of him, but he didn't touch it.

For a long moment he was absolutely motionless and quiet. Then all at once he was up. The door cracked and his feet made heavy, rapid thumps on the steps. As he walked through the long grass going down to the lake, they heard him murmuring, "No, no, no, no, no." A faint luminosity was filtering into the sky from beyond the black trees. They could dimly make him out as he bent beside the canoe, grunted, lifted it over, and let it topple with a metallic whoosh into the tall grass. Then there was the clamor of a paddle dropping onto the aluminum. He spent a long time sighing and cursing over the rope connecting the canoe to the stake, but at last got it untied, went down to the lower end of the canoe, and dragged it across the grass with both hands.

He stopped at the edge of the lake and pushed the canoe past him until it was halfway out onto the water. Standing up, he reached around under his belly, undid his belt, and let his pants drop. Then he sat down in the grass and tugged at the laces of his shoes. A moment later he was standing bare-legged and knock-kneed at the edge of the lake, his belly swaying under his dangling shirttails like a half-filled balloon.

"Cold!" he exclaimed as he splashed into the water. His elbows jerked up and down. His whole body twitched with what looked like childish excitement. He put his arms on the edges of the canoe and it slid from the shore with a squawk and a swish. The canoe rocked dangerously as he rolled into it. They heard the clunk of his knees, the squeak of wet flesh on metal, and then the suck of the paddle drawing back on the still surface. The canoe angled smoothly across the water and was absorbed into the dark reflection of the woods on the far shore.

They crept carefully from their hiding place behind the tree and moved along the edge of the clearing down to the water. The dew on the grass drenched and chilled their legs. The whole time they had been in hiding they had hugged each other against the cold. Morning was nearing. The sky had lightened enough so that only the strongest of the stars were still visible. A luminous mist rose in strands off the wavering surface of the lake. But it was still so dark that they couldn't even make out the faintest glimmer of the canoe. They were standing about ten feet from the man's abandoned trousers, shoes, and socks, not daring to go nearer. They listened for the splash of his oar or the swish of lake water against the hull of the canoe. For a long time they heard nothing. Then, very clearly, but softened by great distance, they heard an "Ah!" and shortly, an "Oh!" Then nothing. They waited, bent with the cold, clutching each other. Nothing. Only the clicking of the lake waves in the reeds and the whisper of insect droppings falling against dead leaves. By dawn there was no trace of the man or his canoe on the clean, glittering water. Dressed once again in his clothes, they set out on the dirt track heading back to civilization, and listened the whole way for the roar of his Jeep coming up behind them.

II

*If I had called, and he had answered
      me,*
*yet would I not believe that he had
      hearkened unto my voice.*
For he breaketh me with a tempest,
*and multiplieth my wounds without
      cause.*
*He will not suffer me to take my
      breath,*
but filleth me with bitterness.
If I speak of strength, lo, he is strong:
*and if of judgment, who shall set me a
      time to plead?*
*If I justify myself, mine own mouth
      shall condemn me:*
*if I say, I am perfect; it shall also prove
      me perverse.*
*Though I were perfect, yet would I not
      know my soul:*
I would despise my life.
                    Job 9:16–21

Dad; or the Builder of Bridges

The young man was carrying his father home in a paper bag. He was on the subway, one of the new trains that didn't roar and clank, but sailed down the tracks going *click, click, click.* Everyone could hear his father's shouts. No one said anything, of course, but the young man caught the glances over the tops of newspapers and under armpits, and saw that even when eyes weren't turned in his direction, ears were. He blushed and wore a patient, weary smile. Every now and then he lowered his lips to make soft noises against the hard brown paper, but his father was inconsolable, screaming as loud as his tiny lungs would let him, not words—his misery was beyond words—but pure, self-centered, world-annihilating grief, pausing only when a sudden wad of phlegm blew in or out of some breathing cavity and he would collapse onto the paper floor, a heap of coughs and wheezes. But only for a minute. Then he would be up again, pounding and kicking the walls of the bag, and screaming with a renewed ferocity. One time, however, the screaming suddenly stopped and the young man heard only a strange, monotonous whisper, that he soon realized was his father gnawing on a fold of paper like a rat.

The young man's mother had hardly been able to bring herself to ask him to take his father. Her sister, whom she hadn't seen in nearly twelve years, was coming to visit. "You know," she said. They were in the kitchen. The old man was in the living room, sitting in his favorite chair, watching TV. "If only he wasn't . . ." She nodded toward the living room. "She and I have so much to talk about . . . I mean, if only you could . . ." The young man did not blame his mother. He knew how much trouble his father had become. It had already occurred to him, several times, that he ought to offer her such a vacation. When he paused a moment before nodding yes, she pleaded with her watery gray eyes, humbly, despising her own neediness, becoming shrunken, feeble, and old. He was amazed at how old both his parents had suddenly become.

The young man kept the bag at his side. On his knees he balanced a pot of chicken stew—his father's favorite dish— prepared that morning by his mother. The young woman sitting next to him must have felt his father's frantic blows (the seats were so narrow), but she never let on until the old man, taking a running start, flung his whole body against the side of the bag and gave her a good poke in the ribs. She winced and edged away without a word.

"I'm sorry," the young man said, shifting the pot to one knee and putting the bag onto the other.

"That's okay," the young woman smiled sympathetically. "Is it your father?" she asked.

The young man nodded and blushed. He blushed easily.

"Mine's just the same."

The young man was grateful for her sympathy and returned her smile, but couldn't think of anything else to say the whole rest of the ride.

Out on the sidewalk, he put the stew pot between his feet, opened the top of the bag, and looked down at his father, who had finally sunk into resentful silence. "Okay," he said. "I'm going to let you out. But don't try to run away, do you hear?"

His father did not respond. He was sitting on the bottom of the bag with his legs straight out in front of him, his back arched like a shoehorn, and his fists clenched defiantly on either side of his thighs. Nevertheless, he did not resist when the young man reached into the bag and pulled him out.

The young man made a sort of seat with both hands and lifted his father until their faces were more or less on the same level. With an affection that was not entirely artificial, he said,

"Okay, I'm going to put you down on the sidewalk. But you stay close to me. You don't know this neighborhood and you might get lost."

"Don't you talk to me like that!" said the old man. "You shit! You baboon! I'll cut off your head if you turn your back on me for two seconds!"

The young man could hardly bear to see his father in such a state. With great tenderness he lowered him to the pavement and, saying, "Come on, Dad," picked up his pot and began to walk away. But the old man stood rigidly where he had been put down, face averted, arms folded tightly across his chest, a statuette of proud fury. The young man was half inclined to keep walking and teach his father a lesson, but just at that moment the subway unleashed another horde of commuters and his father was obscured by swinging shins, spiked heels, and cruising attaché cases. The crowd passed like a puff of fog and the young man saw that his father had not budged, not a fraction of an inch. Then he saw that his father's arms were not folded on his chest, but flung across it, clutching at his sides, as if he were afraid of being separated from himself. As the young man bent down, his father looked him in the eye for the first time, saying weakly, "Where am I? What's happened to me?"

"Don't worry, Dad." The young man hugged the tiny figure against his chest. "I'm with you. I'll take care of you." He kissed his father's balding, golf-ball-sized head and, nestling him in the crook of his arm, carried him down the street.

Part of the reason the young man had not wanted to take his father for the night was that he was ashamed of his life. He lived alone in what had once been the kitchen of a much larger apartment. His bed was a mattress on three long boards. In the mornings he rolled up the mattress and used the boards as a table. He bathed in a metal bucket that stood in front of the sink and kept his clothes in the cupboards where he should have had food. He had no food. His refrigerator did not work and his stove only leaked stinking fumes that were not gas. All of his meals came from the deli on the corner, and sometimes from his mother. She kept him alive with her stews and with the pittance she gave him out of her own salary. She thought he was studying for his engineering exams. The fact was that he had already flunked them three times, but he hadn't been able to tell her. The exams were being held again in a week or two, but he was not studying because he had sold all his books. "Why do you live like this!" he sometimes shouted in the night. But he didn't have an answer. Perhaps it had something to do with his father's condition. His father, who had always been so proud of him, who still bragged about him whenever a friend came to visit. "My son, the builder of bridges," he would say. Neither the young man nor his mother had seen any reason to tell his father their separate truths. The old man had put in sixteen years of overtime so that his son could be an engineer—why give him one more thing to regret? Now, of course, the truth wouldn't mean a thing to him, but still the young man was ashamed—of his life and of the lies he had told. But what could he do?

By the time they reached the apartment his father was emitting perfect little snores, like a zipper going up and down. The young man laid him carefully on a bit of rug, relocked the locks, and hung his coat on a hook. When he turned back the old man was gone. "Oh, Christ, now I've really done it!" the young man said aloud. He began to sweat. His mouth went dry. If he lost his father, his mother would never forgive him.

He turned around and around in a circle, unable to decide where to look first. There were so many cracks, gaps, and holes through which his father could have slipped. The young man shuddered as he thought of the rats that scuttled hungrily inside the walls and of the vicious cat next door that had once blinded a small child. Finally he ran to the end of his kitchen, where three floorboards had turned to crumbly gray powder and dropped into a blackness. The hole could not have been very deep; all that was below him was the basement. But whenever the young man dropped something into the blackness—a chunk of cement or a penny—it was swallowed without a sound, without the faintest click. The young man stuck his head into the hole and shouted, "Dad!" But he might just as well have been shouting into his pillow. "Dad!" The sound was sucked away so fast it hardly reached his ears.

As he drew his head out of the hole, he had the sense that something had just passed very close to his face at a very high speed, leaving behind a pungent earthy smell and the impression of redness and greenness. Then he became aware of a different sort of motion—smaller and horizontal—and looked up to see his father running along the shelf where his solitary plant, a geranium, had once stood. The old man was carrying a fork and muttering under his breath, "Damn! Goddamn it! I don't deserve this!" The young man caught him easily with one hand, but when he drew him off the shelf, the old man swung the fork around and jabbed him in the cheek.

"Watch it, Dad!" The young man twisted the fork out of his father's hands. "You almost got me in the eye."

"That's what I wanted to do, you goon! You twirp! You chicken fart! I'll show you who wears the pants around here! Your days are numbered, my fine young friend! I've got murder in my heart and blood in my eye! . . ."

The young man's father went on in this vein, and worse, for most of the evening. The young man found it particularly difficult because he didn't dare let go of his father again. He paced up and down the narrow kitchen, holding the old man at arm's length, trying to find a way to plug up both ears with his one free hand and arm. He stuck a finger in one ear and attempted to stop up the other with his shoulder, his bicep, a bundled-up coat, a bottle, and even a block of wood—but nothing worked. For a while he stood with one ear up against the wall, but somehow the crumbling mortar only magnified his father's impassioned tirade. The young man was not spared one syllable of it, not one curse or groan. A long lifetime of resentment, envy, humiliation, fear, frustration, and greed poured over him like a river of garbage. "I'm going to split you open and strangle you with your own intestines," his father said. "I'm going to stew you in arsenic and serve you to that whore, that sadistic tyrant, that cannibal in fluffy slippers who brought you into this world!"

The young man heard detailed accounts of his mother's many sins, of her sexual deviance and insufficiencies; he heard the lengthy saga of the joy, wrath, and sorrow of his father's veiny member; he heard of hitherto secret plots and scandals, of torrid, sordid, and just plain bleak scenes involving everyone he knew: his family, his friends, and even himself. Most of what he heard was simple insanity—his mother had never sent anyone a letter bomb and his aunt was not married to a rooster—but some of it, the worst of it, coincided closely enough with his own uneasy imaginings, or cast remembered events in such a startlingly different light that it just might have been true. The young man blushed, turned pale, shouted, and

shed tears. He tried to reason with his father, to comfort or
placate him. He tried threats, silences, and bribes. He offered
him scotch, he offered him his mother's chicken stew, all to no
avail. He grew dizzy with uncertainty and guilt. He thought he
was going crazy. But worst of all he could not stop thinking of
how easy it would be to shut his father up for good; just a quick
twist, a flick of the wrist, a squeeze. At times he actually raised
his hand or felt his fingers tightening. But he resisted. And he
regathered his wits during his father's blessedly frequent bouts
of coughing.

Then all at once it was over. The old man spluttered,
coughed, wheezed, and grew limp. The young man's mother
had told him about this. His father's fits of rage or fear would
go on for hours without slackening an iota and then, all of a
sudden, in the middle of a sentence, he would reach the very
end of exhaustion, and drop into a deep slumber. "The house
could fall down and he wouldn't twitch a nostril," the young
man's mother had said.

He placed the tiny body gently onto a rubber dish drainer
and fell to the floor, writhing in physical and mental agony. His
hand was on fire. His arm convulsed with excruciating spasms
and cramps. His father's words, senseless and otherwise,
swarmed through his mind like an army of roaches.

It is possible that the young man also fell asleep. But
eventually he got up and carefully undressed his father,
putting him into the little blue pajamas that his mother had
given him. Then he lowered him into a drawer, where he had
made a bed of clean dish towels earlier that day. The old man
looked so fragile in his unconscious state, with his tiny feet
sticking out of his pajama pants and his perfect toothpick
fingers resting beside his head. The young man pulled up the
dish-towel blanket and turned away with a shudder.

That night the young man had the strangest dreams. In a
way they weren't dreams at all, but memories resurfacing like
whales on a moonless sea. He remembered the hugeness of his
father's pores. He remembered the meaty smell of his shoulders
and the brown, seething river of his breath. But most of all he
remembered his father's weight, the mass of him, the way his
hulking man's body could immobilize a boy's limbs against the
living-room floor.

Then, in that long hour that immediately precedes night's

sudden shift toward morning, the young man was awoken by something tugging at his toe. He sat up in the dim street glow and saw his father standing in the drawer at the foot of his bed. No sooner did their eyes meet than the old man dropped back onto the folded dish towels with a merry cackle.

The young man was too tired to investigate, so he also lay back. Just as he began to drift toward slumber, his father started pulling on his toes again. The young man sat up and the old man toppled backward in another paroxysm of happy laughter. This time the young man was awake enough to wonder what could be so funny inside the drawer. He leaned forward and his father stood up on the dish towels, saying, "Do it again!"

"Do what?"

"Lie down and sit up!"

There was such a merry glint in his father's eye that the young man did as he was told. And once more his father tumbled backward laughing. The young man couldn't figure out what was going on. When his father had staggered to his feet again, the young man fell back once more and then sat up suddenly. His father collapsed with laughter and the young man himself emitted a low grunt of mirth. The next time he sat up and saw his father's tiny face split with glee, he couldn't help laughing himself. He sat up again, laughing harder this time, and then again, laughing harder and harder, echoed by the diminutive laughter of his father. And in a like manner, rising and toppling, father and son laughed through the night's longest hour. And even longer.

The Invitation

She had been given a place of honor beside the great man. Every now and then he would lean over, envelop her with one arm, press his huge rough cheek against hers, and call out to whoever was listening—and everyone was—"My little girl! Isn't she wonderful!" For some reason this infuriated her, even though it seemed to make everyone else terribly happy. They smiled. They nodded. They said, "She certainly is!" and "You sure are lucky to have one like her."

Perhaps it was the way he smelled that made his proclamations so difficult to bear. Despite his incredible transformation, which was the whole reason for this celebration, he still stank like a slaughterhouse dumpster. She could hardly breathe from the smell. It was as if a foul rag had been shoved down her throat. But nobody else seemed to notice. They all laughed and chatted with the great man, and complimented him on his astonishing recovery. Great beauties leaned across the table, granting him (and her) views down the glorious caverns beneath their necklines—not a wince or a wrinkled nose among them. The only sign she saw that anyone else even noticed the smell was that the people sharing the great man's table seemed inordinately fastidious, covering the lower halves of their faces with their napkins after nearly every bite. But that was all and it was nothing she could be sure of.

Or perhaps it was because she wasn't his daughter. Every time he leaned over and made his proclamation, she wanted to say, "I'm not your little girl, I'm your daughter-in-law!" But she couldn't do it, not in the face of all that good cheer and admiration, and not after his transformation, which, even if it hadn't been complete, was nonetheless a miraculous improvement and a testimony to the great man's extraordinary strength of will. A couple of times she even caught herself calling him "Dad." She couldn't understand how she could have made such a mistake. But everyone seemed touched by it. They smiled. They said, "You have such a wonderful relationship!" "Isn't he the most marvelous man!"

She looked to her husband for rescue, but he was as bad as the rest. Whenever she tried to convey her agony to him with her eyes, he would only gaze back at her lovingly and purse his lips in a silent kiss. When the great beauties came to compliment the great man, they would always put their hands on her husband's shoulder. One of them even massaged his neck. And as they leaned across the table, he would leer unabashedly at the wonders he could glimpse through the dangling armholes of their dresses.

Later, when they were dancing, she said to him, "Isn't this awful!"

"Oh, I don't know," he replied. "I think it's pretty amazing." He lowered his voice and drew his lips closer to her ear. "I mean, have you been looking around at all the people in this room?" He jerked his chin in the direction of a celebrated actress who was swaying in the arms of an elder statesman. "I've never seen so many famous faces in one place in all my life. I had no idea my father knew all these people. I'm amazed we were invited."

"What are you talking about!" she said. "You're his son! Of course you were invited. It would have been shocking if you weren't."

"But you have to admit, we're hardly of the caliber of the rest of the people in this room." He stopped dancing and took a step away from her. "Look at me. I'm not wearing a suit, my tie's got spots on it, and my socks don't even match." He tugged at the knees of his pants so that she could see one green sock and one red one.

She was astonished to see her husband demean himself like this. For years he had hated his father and everything the old man stood for. When they got the invitation he had only wanted to accept out of pity. "Look, the poor guy's life has been hell for the last decade," he had said. "Now it seems as if things are finally starting to pick up for him. I mean, he's practically his old self again. I can't just turn my back on that. He'd be so hurt if I didn't come."

As her husband stood in front of her pinching the knees of his pants, one of the great beauties came up to him and tapped him on the shoulder. Turning up his palms and tilting his head to indicate helplessness, he let himself be swept off across the dance floor.

No sooner had he vanished into the swirl of opulent bodies than she felt a tap on her own shoulder. It was her mother-in-law, a stout, pigeon-breasted woman, with very small eyes that were as dark and unreadable as nail heads.

"I'm glad I found you," the old woman said. "Are you having a good time?"

"Oh, yes!" said the daughter-in-law. "It's a splendid show you've put on here. Everyone seems to be having such a wonderful time."

Her mother-in-law looked at her strangely for a moment, then said, "Yes. It's almost like the old days, isn't it?"

At this remark the young woman remembered what an ordeal the great man's decline had been for his wife. The truth was that the young woman had always despised her mother-in-law, in part for her ruling-class affectations, but mostly for the way she let herself be humiliated and abused by the great man without even a murmur of protest, as if her submissiveness were somehow ennobling. But now the young woman could only think of the enormous toll the years had extracted from her mother-in-law, who had herself once been a great beauty. Taking hold of her hand, she said, "You must be very happy."

The old woman scowled. "Yes. Well, I've made my choices, I suppose. In any event, it's too late to change things." Drawing her hand from the daughter-in-law's loose grasp, she said, "Quick, come with me! I want to show you something."

She turned and plunged into the idly chatting crowd on the edge of the dance floor. The young woman followed.

The ballroom was much larger than it had first seemed. In a moment they had left the merrymakers behind and were moving across a vast dim floor, empty except for the occasional wandering drunk or motionless couple. At the far end of the room there was a grand staircase that rose to a dark mezzanine. The steps were rather taller than the young woman had expected and she tripped twice because the tight skirt of her evening dress would not let her spread her legs far enough apart. On the first landing a woman in a full pink gown stood with her face against the wall. As the young woman drew closer she realized that there was a man standing in front of the woman and that the woman's gown had been hiked up in front so that he could reach under and put his hands on her buttocks. The man and the woman were pressed so tightly together that, as the young woman sidled past, she could not make out either of their faces. "Hurry," said her mother-in-law, in a much too loud voice. "I'm doing this for your good, not mine." As the young woman continued to climb, the stairs got darker and darker until finally she was just lifting and lowering her legs in a perfect blackness.

She was striding down what looked like a long hospital corridor past small clusters of men in black uniforms. They were soldiers, their eyes hollow from lack of sleep, their brows glossy with anxious sweat. Several of them had automatic rifles slung over their shoulders or cradled in their arms. The hall was utterly silent. Not one of the men breathed a word. As she passed they looked at her, some with hostile squints, others with boredom, as if she were just another shadow passing along the wall. But a few of them watched her with a pathetic longing, as if they thought she was the last woman they would ever see and they had something urgent and profoundly inexpressible to communicate to her.

"Has there been another bombing?" she asked her mother-in-law. "Why haven't all the guests been informed?"

"No. Nothing like that. Just be quiet and hurry."

The corridor ended in a lofty-ceilinged room, illuminated only by a blue glow pouring through tall French doors. The gilt frames of huge pictures glinted dimly on the walls. A chandelier tinkled overhead and thick carpets muffled their footsteps as they hurried toward and then through the doors, out onto a moonlit terrace.

Her mother-in-law gave her hand a squeeze before letting go. "There he is, my darling girl. Run to him."

"Who?" she said. "Where?" The terrace was empty and utterly silent, despite the party going on elsewhere in the house.

"There!" Her mother-in-law pointed down the wide marble steps to where the silhouette of a tall thin man stood beside a dry fountain. "Fly to him now, before it's too late!" Then louder so that the man could also hear: "Fly, my darlings!"

As the young woman hurried down the steps, she recognized her husband. His tie was loosened and his shirttails hung out of his trousers. He was panting heavily, as if he had just stopped running. There was a streak of mud—or was it blood?—running down his temple onto his cheek. As she drew up to him, she smelled the choking stink of his father.

"I'm sorry, my love," he said, taking hold of her hand.

"For what?"

"For all of that. For before."

"How did you get here so fast? What's going on?"

"I can't tell you." He looked anxiously over his shoulder. "I've been doing something. For quite some time now. But I can't tell you what it is. We don't have time." He pulled on her hand, leading her around the fountain. "We've got to run. My father's not better. He's worse than ever. He's been doing the most abominable things. We've got to get out of here as fast as we can."

Behind the fountain the lawn sloped steeply and she had no choice but to run, just to keep from falling. Her high heels spun off into the dark and soon her dress no longer bound her thighs. She was amazed that she could run so well at so late an hour, after having had so much to drink. The cool lawn sped ever faster beneath her feet, her tattered stockings fluttered at her ankles, and for a while she felt there was no limit to her physical capability. But then the lawn ended. They had reached the edge of the forest. "This way," said her husband, still pulling her by the hand. "Quickly!" Thorns tore at her clothes. Sharp twigs gouged her feet. An unseen branch caught her on the shoulder and knocked her flat onto her back. Her husband was kneeling beside her. "I know it's hard," he said. "But

we've got to hurry. You'll understand soon. Soon it will be all
over." She had never seen such urgency in him. His eyes
gleamed as if glazed with mercury. He lifted her to her feet and
then hurried beside her, supporting her with a steady arm
across her shoulders. The sharp smacks of machine-gun fire
sounded from the direction of the house. Spotlights strafed the
tops of the trees, filling the woods with silent streaking balls of
green flame. "Just a little farther," said her husband. And then
at last they stepped onto a paved road where a silver limousine
glinted under the hurtling lights.

"Is that for us?" she asked.

"Yes," said her husband. "We made it."

As they crossed the road, the limousine door flew open.
Hands pulled them into the perfectly black interior. She sank
into an embrace of soft leather, with her back to the driver, and
the car began to accelerate soundlessly, without the faintest
vibration. She waited for someone to speak, but no one said a
word, and she too kept quiet, assuming there was some good
reason for the silence. The car was moving at a fantastic speed.
Through the rear window she watched the road dissolve into a
red-tinted swirl. Every now and then a beam of ocher streetlight
swept across a woman's cheek, a man's bright cuff, or a glittery
shoe lying on its side. But in between the darkness in the car
was so deep it seemed to press upon her eyes. A man was
sitting next to her. Perhaps he was asleep. She felt his warmth
against her thigh, and the smooth silk of his suit. After a while
she found that she could lie back in her seat as far as she
wanted. A heaviness was settling in her aching limbs. Soon she
was stretched out flat. And then she too was asleep.

When she awoke she called her husband's name.

A woman's voice whispered, "Shhh! He's asleep."

"Oh," said the young woman. She was still too sleepy
herself to know what to say next.

"He needs his rest," said the voice.

"Yes," she said.

After a long pause the woman said, "He's a great man."

"Who?"

"Your husband. You're very lucky."

"Thank you." She liked to hear her husband praised, although "great" was not an adjective she would ever have
applied to him. He was a good man. He tried hard. But he was

always so full of doubt. She wondered what this woman knew about her husband that, perhaps, she did not. As she drew her breath to speak, the woman cut her off: "Be quiet! We're coming to a checkpoint."

Looking out the tinted windows, she saw that the limousine was now moving so slowly that two soldiers were able to walk right along beside it. One of them held an automatic rifle leveled at his waist and the other was jotting something in a notebook. "Don't worry," said the woman. "The driver will take care of everything." As the limousine advanced, the world outside the windows grew more and more brilliantly illuminated. Tanks and half-tracks loomed out of the obscurity. A machine-gun installation. A white clapboard farmhouse with all its windows glowing. And men. Everywhere there were men in black uniforms and white helmets, some of them standing as still as signposts, others playing cards at folding tables, or strolling with their ears cocked to portable radios. The actual checkpoint was lit to a more than noontime brilliance by the beams of four searchlights. Other searchlights cast long ovals back and forth across distant fields.

Only when the car had eased to a halt and she heard the hum of the driver's window going down did the young woman notice that the inside of the car was also bathed with light. She saw her husband directly across from her, not asleep but up on his elbows, hollow-eyed, frowning, unable to meet her gaze. The mark on his cheek was lipstick, she saw, not blood or mud. A woman, one of the great beauties, was stretched beside him, her arm on his shoulder, her long fingers tucked into the collar of his shirt. She was grinning with the shamelessness of one who was thoroughly drunk. Catching the young woman's eye, she lifted her index finger to her mouth, puckered her lips, and emitted a long "Shhhhhh!" Then her finger dropped and traced a line from her bust to her knees. In an instant, the whole front of her dress had fallen apart and the lanky glory of her nakedness shone in the ocher brilliance.

"Oh, God!" said the young woman's husband, throwing back his head and covering his face with his hands. The brilliance was fading. The limousine had already begun to slide away from the checkpoint. There was a long darkness, then a flash of streetlight: The empty dress of the woman, of the great beauty, lay crumpled on the floor.

The young woman could not stand to be in the car another instant, but from the speed of the moon crashing silently through the trees, she knew she could not escape. "You can go this way," said a voice, a man's voice. It was the man who had been sleeping next to her. She had never even glanced at his face. "Right here," he said. His voice was deep and kind. She felt a strong hand take hold of her wrist. Another touched the small of her back and turned her toward the front of the car. "There you are," he said. Something gave way beneath her fingertips, and she found herself in a brighter place, on her hands and knees. A terrible stench enveloped her.

"No. Don't go. Please." A new voice. A man's voice. She lifted her head.

Her father-in-law was sitting at the wheel, gripping it tightly with both hands. She noticed—or rather, remembered—that he was really a very small man. This was a fact that she had always had difficulty grasping, that always, somehow, confused her. But the truth was that he was so small he had to sit on a pillow to see over the dashboard, and the car's pedals had to have blocks taped to them so that he could reach them with his feet.

"I'm sorry you had to see that," he said, not taking his eyes off the road. "He's my own flesh and blood, but I didn't want you to have any illusions about him. It was the only way."

He patted the seat beside him. "Come on. Keep me company. It's lonely up here. I'm afraid I'm going to fall asleep."

They were driving across a wide plain. A mile or so ahead a tongue of mist, silver in the moonlight, stretched across the highway, and beyond that she could make out the dark flank of the mountains.

"Come on," he said. "I just need a little companionship."

She saw the radiant eyes of animals transfixed by the headlights. Small green bushes turned gray as they shot past into the darkness.

"If it will help," he said, "I'll apologize. I suppose you know that I'm not really any better. What he told you is true. My life is a complete mess."

For a long time she neither moved nor spoke. Then, clutching at the ruins of her dress, she slid onto the edge of the seat.

"Good," he said. "Thanks. Talk to me. We've still got a long way to go."

"Where are we going?" she said.

"Where?" he asked, as if he found her question highly original, though perhaps a little foolish. "You might say that we're going to another party. Yes, to another party. But this one you're going to enjoy. I promise you. I give you my word of honor." He turned to her and smiled.

What Makes You Think You Deserve This?

He had come to them to ask for money. They were his mother's friends. He didn't know them very well, and hadn't known that they would be so old. They were immeasurably old, the man and the woman, preserved by their immense wealth, like butterflies in a glass case. That was not something he had remembered about them. But then, he didn't have a good memory for faces. He had always thought of himself as someone who cared about people. But no. It was true. He simply cut them off. All his life he had discarded friends like yesterday's newspapers. "See you soon," he'd say, then never see them again.

Still, they were cordial enough. They seemed to know what he had come for. The man, the husband, was seated in a chair. He lifted one arm high into the air and waved, as if he were on a boat pulling away from the dock. She met him at the door. "Oh, we were just talking about you," she said.

"Nothing bad, I hope," he replied, proud, under the circumstances, that he could muster any trace of wit.

"What was that?" She thumped the side of her head, as if to shake something loose.

He spoke louder: "Nothing bad, I hope."

"I'm sorry?"

"I said, *nothing bad,* I hope."

"Please forgive me." She was smiling. Her head was tilted expectantly.

"It doesn't matter."

"I'm afraid you'll have to speak up. My aid's on the fritz." She thumped the side of her head once again.

"I said, *it doesn't matter.*"

Her smile faded. She looked at him curiously, for a very long time.

He was surprised at how many people they had working in their home. The hallway was crowded with men and women in dark business suits. Youngish men and women. In their mid-forties. At the height of their careers. They smiled and nodded as they passed the old woman, but she appeared not to notice. "We've heard so much about you," she was saying.

"Nothing bad, I hope." How could he have said that again? And how was he going to ask for money with all of these people around? He had to get a grip on himself.

"Oh, no, no. We're surrounded by your admirers."

Now he was in the bathroom. He'd walked in the door and practically the first thing he'd said was, "Where's your bathroom?" That was a mistake. That was definitely not the way to handle these venerable people. He looked at himself in the mirror: a rumpled man in his mid-forties. Stains on his dove gray shirt, no tie, the embarrassment of his pink dome concealed only by a mat of lacquered strands brushed leftward from his temple. In his hands he held his penis, which was surprisingly long, brown, and of no particular shape.

"I just want you to know," said the man, "that we've signed all the papers. It's all taken care of. So you have nothing to worry about."

He, the younger man, the supplicant, felt momentarily grateful. But something was wrong. He had forgotten something. He couldn't quite think of what.

"Let's drink to your success," said the man, who was lying on his back on an antique invalid's couch, made of iron bars and varnished oak, with big, white baby-carriage wheels. He was holding a glass straight up in the air and the younger man didn't see how he was going to be able to drink from it without spilling all over his face.

The woman came up to the younger man with a sweaty glass of clear liquid. He took it greedily. He was very thirsty.

"We love you very much," she said, giving his hand a squeeze.

"I love you too," he said, blushing deeply. She knew he was lying.

"I hear you've come to ask for money," said the cook, a sturdy, pink woman with the solid buttocks of a farm animal, and skin as smooth as a baby's. Her voice was dull, as if she were talking in her sleep, except it had a cruelish inflection.

"I've already got it," he said proudly.

"No, you don't." She didn't look around. She was cutting chunks of raw beef. "Have they told you when you're going to get it?"

"No," he answered. This is what he had forgotten to ask.

"Have they told you how much?"

"No." He had forgotten to ask this as well. Money talk always embarrassed him.

He didn't understand the next thing she said, something about how they couldn't be trusted. Then she said, "It all depends upon me." She still wasn't looking at him. Her voice was still dull and cruel. But he realized that she wanted him to come into her.

After that there was some confusion. The cook was lying face-down on the wet, concrete kitchen floor. He was in her, very close to orgasm, but something was not right. "No, that's not it," she said. And then the old woman was standing in the doorway with her hands on her hips. "Look." She pointed with a gnarled finger. He looked where the old woman was pointing and saw that the seam between the cook's buttocks was smooth and pink and completely without blemish. But that was irrelevant. He was so close to an orgasm. He wanted the old woman to go away. She grabbed his wrist with her bony hand and said, "Come with me."

The old man was sitting in a chair now, at a huge table. He raised his glass and said in a hearty voice, "Hail the master of the house and manor." The younger man was touched by how completely this couple had taken him in. There were tears in his eyes. But he couldn't pay attention to what they were saying. The cook was crouched under the table, between his legs, performing fellatio, although neither of the old people seemed to notice. A vast meal had been laid out in front of him: buckets of soup, fish with their heads on, pineapples, coconuts, and something long and pink that twitched as if it were still alive. The old couple had not even lifted a crumb onto their plates, but the younger man had already had three helpings. "Eat! Eat!" they said. "You're still a growing boy." He wanted to say something about how he was no longer growing, but his mouth was packed tight and he was lost in the cook's warm, long throat. He kept spilling things all over the floor, big things: chicken legs, doughnuts, tomatoes. They made loud noises as they fell, but no one seemed to notice. He just hoped they wouldn't bend over and see.

The old woman was leading him by the wrist through the basement of her home. It was very dark. The floors were littered with garbage, gravel, broken glass. Oozing black beards of bacteria hung down the walls and water gathered in puddles on the floor, running in rills amid the garbage. All around them, mostly obscured by darkness, loomed the great flanks of machines, badly rusted, lumpy with the same oozing growth as the walls. After a while he began to suspect that he was actually walking through his own guts, but she explained that they were inside a ship that had spent many years submerged beneath the North Atlantic. "That's why it's all such a mess," she said. Now that she'd mentioned it, he could see the long rusty drive shaft that was connected to the ship's propeller. At one point they had to slide under the shaft and over the top of a wide machine. The space was very narrow and they had to lie flat on their backs. Cold water soaked up through their clothing, gravel dug into their spines. But it wasn't too bad really. When he had finally lowered himself to the floor on the other side of the machine, he saw that the old woman was already halfway up a slimy and badly corroded ladder. He followed her up into the open air.

"All of this will be yours," she was saying. They were on a very high hill, perhaps a mountain, and could see for hundreds of miles in all directions to the point where the blue of the earth blended into the blue of the sky. The sun was out. A strong wind was whipping their hair and the grass at their feet. He watched as tall clouds drifted toward them, pushing blue shadows over the rising and falling green of the land. "Enjoy it!" she said. She had to shout because of the wind. "You don't have to be ashamed. You're rich now! It's a wonderful thing!" Directly in front of them, along the edge of a lake, was a city that looked like a heap of cigarette ash on a lush carpet of moss. In the middle of the city there was a huge white building in the shape of a woman's leg. It was still under construction. Tiny people were crawling all over it like ants. They were dangling from threads that were swept into graceful arcs by the wind. On the far side of the city there was a mountain tall enough to be powdered with snow. And beyond that: the blue earth and the blue sky.

"How long until all of this is mine?" he asked.

"What was that?" she said, thumping the side of her head.

"I'm sorry," he said.

"Please forgive me," she said.

He shouted into the wind.

III

I have heard of thee by the hearing of
the ear;
but now mine eye seeth thee:
wherefore I abhor myself,
and repent in dust and ashes.
                                    Job 42:5–6

Loyal Channa

I picked the dead leaves off of trees. That was my first job at the palace. Not bad for a boy of seven. I would clamber up to the flimsiest heights with a hooked pole, pull the rubbery branch tips toward me, and pluck off any brown or yellow leaves. Then I would rub the leaves between my hands until they had shredded or turned to powder, and let them go on the wind, which would carry them to where they belonged, to this world of death, pain, and dissatisfaction.

You may think that climbing to the heights of the ancient trees that surround the palace was too dangerous a job for so young a child. It was. My predecessor was a boy of nine, who had been plucking leaves for more than half his life and whose arms had grown long like a monkey's. He used to brag that he never needed a hook. He would climb out onto a branch, let it bend until he was hanging completely upside down, and then just reach out his giant's arm and pluck. Well, you can imagine what happens to a boy who hangs upside down from branches that are skinnier than a snake's tongue. I have heard that he is still a beggar in the Rumination District, where he walks like a spider on his long arms, dragging his withered body across the mud and the filth.

But falling was not the greatest danger. "Always be sure to

grind the leaves until they are nothing, until they go back to the earth and the air from which they came." This is what my uncle, the royal Garden Master, told me. "If one dead leaf enters the presence of the prince, even if he doesn't notice it, you will be made to wish you had never been born." And this was true. Shortly after I began spending my days in the trees, one of the other leaf pickers, a boy my own age, pulled too hard with his pole and broke a branch. He tugged and twisted, but wasn't strong enough to tear the branch off. What he should have done was gone to my uncle, who had saws and axes and giant shears on sticks for just this sort of thing. But the boy must have been afraid. (It is a foolish fear that fears the lesser evil more than the greater.) The following morning, it was King Suddhodana himself who noticed that the shadow of death had entered the lustrous green of his son's garden. That evening, before the sun had touched the horizon, my uncle, the two other leaf pickers, and I were made to watch as a team of bullocks tore off the foolish boy's limbs, one at a time.

You would be astonished at how many leaves die, even in so lush and well-tended a garden as the palace's. Thousands every day and many more thousands in drought years. I would scramble up and down tree after tree from the first cold light of morning to the last, dusty beam of sunset. I ate with the squirrels and slept with the owls. It was not a bad life. The food was plentiful, both the fruit and nuts I would gather for myself and the prince's leavings, which my uncle would get from the women who cooked the prince's breakfast. And I liked sleeping in the trees. In the hot hours of the afternoon I would climb high into the green shade, where a breeze always fluttered the leaves, and wedge myself next to a thick bough, and feel the tree sway me gently like a strong and tender mother. To my boy's heart this was life's greatest pleasure. But one such nap nearly cost me my life.

It was in the cooling part of the summer when the trees grow weary and cast off the heaviest of their leaves. During these weeks I worked so hard that I never had time to eat and I got so tired that sometimes when I had stretched full length along a branch to reach out with my hook, I would put my head down and fall asleep, right there, balanced on a limb no thicker than my wrist. This happened many times, often when I was at

the very top of a tree. Only the saints of my family could have
kept me from falling. But one day they too must have grown
exhausted and gone to sleep. I was never supposed to be in a
garden when the prince was there. In the mornings while he
amused himself in the Lotus Garden or on the Field of Heroes,
I would pick the Water Forest and make sure that I was well
gone before he came there for his afternoon lessons. But this
day, over the very spot where the prince would sit to receive
instruction in singing, I fell deeply asleep and did not awake
until I was falling through the air. I will tell you, even though
I was awake I was still dreaming. My fall lasted a very long
time, long enough for me to wonder at this strange green and
black and white river that was rushing past me, up into the sky.
Fortunately my arms never slept. The river vanished and I was
dangling a finger's length above the ground, eye to eye with
the prince.

The tutor, as frightened as I was, had already begun shouting
for the guards. But the prince, who was exactly my age, was
delighted. "What a wonderful animal! Is it a monkey? I have
never seen a monkey without fur before. Oh, Siravati, you
never told me that there were monkeys without fur!" The tutor
could only mutter breathlessly between shouts, "Yes, Prince
Siddhartha . . . Well, you see, Prince Siddhartha . . . That is to
say . . ."

Although I too had had a moment of befuddlement, I had
now recovered my wits, dropped from the tree, and started
running. As I splashed into a rushing brook, a guard ran up
behind me, grabbed a hank of my hair in his fist, and yanked
me backward, nearly snapping my neck. I screamed in pain
and instantly a second guard cupped his hand over my mouth,
but it was too late. The prince had seen and had also begun to
scream. "What is happening? The poor monkey! Please, Siravati, make them stop!"

"Fools!" shouted the tutor, who had now regained his
senses. "Let him go, you fools!" The guards immediately put
me down and began stroking and kissing me as if I were their
own child. "That was just a laugh," the tutor explained.
"You've heard them shrieking like that in the trees. That's the
way they laugh when they are happy."

The tutor was pale and breathless and looked as if he were

going to faint, but the boy seemed perfectly content with the explanation. "Look, he is tame!" the prince exclaimed. "He's not running away. Is he my pet? May I keep him?"

The guards cast worried glances between themselves. The tutor stuttered and finally said, "We must ask your father. I believe this monkey must have escaped from the royal menagerie. Perhaps your father intends him for another purpose."

Seeing a way out, I fell to my knees in front of the young prince and kissed his manicured foot.

"Oh, he is a wonderful creature!" exclaimed the prince. "He is practically human! I am sure my father will let me keep him."

I was gently entreated by the guards, with hardly more than a feather's prodding, to accompany them back to the palace. Once inside the palace, however, they threw me to the ground, chained my ankles to my neck, and locked me in a dungeon with a mad old man who was covered with sores that he would pick at with his teeth and suck.

Later that day the tutor and the Minister of the Nursery went before the king to explain how the prince had glimpsed me as I was trying to sneak out of the garden after tardily completing my work, and how he had taken what the king might find to be a somewhat inconvenient fancy to me. Suddhodana could not understand why his subordinates were so worried. His child's every wish was simply to be granted. Henceforth I would be Prince Siddhartha's plaything, and that was that. However, his majesty emphasized that I was to be given strict instructions about what I could and couldn't say and told that if I erred by so much as a syllable, my tongue would be yanked from my mouth. The minister then mentioned the unfortunate complication that, because of my nakedness, my matted hair, and my general filth, the prince had concluded I was a monkey. After many hours' deliberation, the minister was authorized to tell the prince that the tutor had made a mistake and that I was in fact a boy. I was immediately taken from the dungeon, bathed, barbered, and dressed in clothes nearly as fine as the prince's.

The Minister of the Nursery, whose name was Vaharadas, gave me my instructions as I sat at a table spread with more food than I had eaten in all of my seven years put together. I did not know what any of it was, so I took a bite from each of twenty or thirty plates. As I ate, Vaharadas told me what I had already heard rumors of from my uncle and the other leaf pickers.

When the prince had only just been born, that old schemer Kala Devala, the king's chief sage and prognosticator, took one look at the infant, smiled, and then began to weep. When the king asked him why he was behaving so strangely, he answered, "I am smiling because I foresee that this child shall become a perfect being, a buddha. And I am crying because I shall not live to hear his teaching." It is not clear what Kala Devala hoped to accomplish with this prophecy, because everyone knew the king wanted his son to become a fierce warrior and ruler. Suddhodana immediately sent for eight more sages and asked them to examine the infant prince's every bone and birthmark. Now these poor sages were in a fine pickle. If they disappointed the king they faced banishment or worse, but if they disappointed Kala Devala they would have to live under his curse for the rest of their days. Most of them were sensibly equivocal, telling the king that if Siddhartha decided to remain in the world he would become a great ruler, and if he decided to give up the world he could become a buddha. Only Kondanna was foolish enough to take Kala Devala's side. He told the king that the young prince would see four signs: an old man, a sick man, a dead man, and an ascetic, then he would give up the world and become a perfect being. Kala Devala smiled, but the king roared like a gutted lion and chased all of the sages from his chambers. Kala Devala was, of course, invincible, but Kondanna was never seen again.

The king had a quite natural ambivalence toward sages— their prophecies were, after all, the only restraints on his power. It was his general policy to act as if those predictions were only as prescient as a thief was honest—which was probably true. But when it came to the preservation of his lineage, he didn't want to take chances. He decided that the simplest course of action was to have Prince Siddhartha brought up in a world free of all traces of corruption and pain. He banished all ascetics from the palace and its grounds, as well as anyone with a gray hair, a wrinkle, a limp, or a running sore. All flowers were to be dug out of the earth and replaced before they could shed a petal, and the trees, as I have told you, were to be kept free of dead and dying leaves.

I made a mistake as I listened to Vaharadas's account of these

events. The leaf pickers never tired of laughing at the folly of
the king and I assumed that such an attitude was general
among the palace staff. However, when I casually suggested
that everyone would be saved a lot of trouble if the king were
simply reminded that he himself would one day be an old man,
a sick man, and a dead man, Vaharadas grabbed hold of my
hair and thrust the point of his dagger against my throat.
"Little Channa," he said, "if you want to live five seconds in
this palace, you must realize that Prince Siddhartha's is not the
only innocence that must be protected." I did not know what
he meant at the time, but I was soon to learn that a king whose
every whim was instantly obeyed never bothered to consider
anything very carefully and thus could be kept deeply in the
dark about the precise details of his omnipotence.

So I became the prince's plaything. Every morning I was
brought to him in the Field of Heroes. We would run together,
or ride elephants, or stand on our heads or hands, or do any
number of gymnastic feats. But what the prince enjoyed more
than anything was climbing trees. I taught him how to grab
handfuls of slender branches and stick his head out above the
treetops, and how to leap from tree to tree so that we could
cross the garden without ever touching the ground. Vaharadas
did not like such dangerous play, but the prince loved it, so
Vaharadas was helpless. I was to be the prince's constant
companion for three times seven years, and even when we
were both young men—though I was never properly to become
a man—he would sometimes turn to me, give his chin an
upward toss, and we would spend hours conversing in the
whispering green.

It was the isolation of treetops that the prince loved most. I
soon learned that he could not bear the company of his
caretakers. He may have been the very meaning of the word
naive, but he was no fool. He knew that virtually every
sentence spoken in his presence was a lie. How could he not!
The world as Vaharadas and the other tutors and servants
presented it to him was insane. The king had not simply
decreed that sickness and death be banished from the palace,
but that they not even be alluded to in front of his son. So when
the prince had a fever he was told that some peculiar wind was
causing it to be winter and summer at the same time, a lie that
all of his nurses, tutors, and servants would substantiate by

pretending to shiver and sweat as he did. Once when he asked his fencing master why it was important to drive his sword into his opponent's breast, he was told, "So that you can touch his heart. You know that when you touch a woman's heart she falls in love with you. It is the same with your enemy." I couldn't participate in such silliness. It was against my nature. And I could tell that the prince hated it. He could see the glee in his informants' eyes as they tortured him with inanity. He knew, on some unarticulated level, that they were taking vengeance for their fear and humiliation. This is how the evil that sustained the prince's innocence also corrupted it. When he would ask me questions, I wouldn't tell him the truth, but I wouldn't lie either. I would play stupid. And for this alone his respect for me grew to ludicrous proportions. "You may be a fool," he would tell me, "but at least you know you are a fool, and for that reason you are the wisest person in the world."

Vaharadas was outraged by my closeness to his charge. I am sure that he thought I was poisoning the prince against him, but that was hardly necessary. When it came to the prince's opinion of Vaharadas, there was no more potent poison than the man himself. The prince despised him. When Vaharadas would linger behind a column or outside a door, eavesdropping on our conversation, the prince would say, "Channa, do you smell that foul odor? If I didn't know Vaharadas was off napping in his cell, I would swear he was right behind me. What a stink!" Once when Vaharadas had followed us into the trees and lodged himself on a branch directly below us, the prince carefully and wordlessly positioned himself—even I had no idea what he was doing—and defecated on the minister's upturned ear. Vaharadas was so furious that his hands and feet left black scorches on the tree bark, but there was nothing he could do other than withdraw in total silence while the prince cackled like a monkey. Vaharadas's term as Minister of the Nursery expired on the prince's eleventh birthday, but I am sure he still dreams obsessively of taking revenge on his former charge. With me, however, it is another matter. He must sleep quite happily when he dreams of me.

The king had always dismissed what Vaharadas told him about me as the patently envious vituperation it was. However, shortly before his term expired, Vaharadas took a new tack and finally won the king's sympathy. He argued that my relationship with the prince had become indecent. I was a slave but I was being treated as the friend and equal of the heir to the crown. Vaharadas thought that my role ought to be more clearly defined, and made a proposition that the king thought reasonable. I was only a month away from my own eleventh birthday when I was brought before the king and told that henceforth I would be the Servant of Prince Siddhartha's Private Chambers. This was a promotion of sorts, but one with exact and severe strictures, chief of them being that, since the prince would one day be entertained by his courtesans and wife in my presence, I would have to be unmanned. And so, as you have no doubt noticed, I am an old man with a boy's voice. And my wrinkled body is as hairless as an infant's. Power gives and power takes away.

I had no choice but to submit to the king's decree. My uncle assured me that this submission would, if I played my cards right, ultimately make me the most powerful figure in the palace. But I will tell you what I told him: I don't care about power. I nearly died under the knife, and many times after I wanted to die. But I will also tell you that I no longer particularly resent what was done to me. My career has ended following a vastly different course than anyone expected. Looking back on it all from this pleasant garden, I can truly say that I am content with my lot. I have been a watcher, not a participator, and that has had its advantages.

The king gave his son the world of bliss, but the boy knew only misery. I knew what was wrong, but it wasn't my place to say. It was this: The prince knew that half of everything he believed was untrue, but he didn't know which half. The result was that he lived in perpetual uncertainty. I think he worried every morning that the sun was not going to come up. He worried endlessly. He was moody, suspicious, and cruel. Sometimes he would climb into a tree to sulk, and such was the power of his unhappiness that the tree's shadow would not move until he came down.

His only joys were music, dance, painting, and lovemaking—sensual exercises that were complete unto themselves, whose full beauty was open even to the innocence of a child. And, indeed, his accomplishments in all of the arts vastly exceeded those of his teachers; in singing especially—he could lift his voice so high it would make the bells ring and could lower it

until the earth rumbled. Artists and courtesans accepted him as
one of their own and did not mock him with twisted logic or
hollow praise. Only in their presence did he attain anything
resembling his natural stature. The rest of the time he felt
stunted, stupid, and perverse.

Finally, in his eighteenth year, his father built him a pleasure
garden half a day's ride from Kapilavastu. Here the prince
found the only real happiness he was ever to know under his
father's sway. In a gilded hall, beneath a ceiling so lofty that it
was sometimes obscured by clouds, the greatest artists of the
world were gathered together for the prince's enjoyment. The
king sent off caravans and sailing ships to the very limits of the
inhabited earth to bring back poets, jugglers, women, and
painters of the most peculiar styles, hues, and physical con-
structions. There was a muscular poet, with smoky hair all over
his body, whose chanting was like the smashing of rocks. And
a quiet, small woman, the luminous brown of the leaves I used
to shred between my hands, who would paint pictures of
nothing. (Hers were the images the prince loved most; he said
they were portraits of his soul.) There were giantesses, as pale,
slender, and sad as death candles, who would coo like owls in
the prince's arms. And sturdy zebra women, with great buttocks and laughing mouths, who would ride the prince around
on their shoulders and throw him back and forth between
them. In this place, amid these wild people, the prince would
lose himself for solid weeks of frenzied ecstasy. But such joy
destroys itself. And in the end the prince would flee to the
palace to sleep for days and arise with no more than a cinder for
a soul. Often he would pace the palace ramparts and I would
hover next to him, sure that he was about to leap off.

I will be honest with you. I was far from the great friend the
prince thought I was. How could I be? I was no different than
any other servant. I too suffered humiliation and fear so that
the prince could live in a luxury he never recognized. And my
suffering wasn't only for myself. In the monsoon season of my
twelfth year at the palace, the Tree of the Gautama's Eternal
Ascendancy got root rot and toppled across the Field of Heroes.
This was such an ill omen that all the sages immediately fled
the capital and did not show their faces for weeks. The only one
left to blame was my uncle, the Garden Master. So in a
magnificent ceremony before the whole court, he was declared

disloyal, hamstrung, and thrown out of the palace. He had to sell his fine house on Transcendence Street and move into an arcade in the Rumination District. I gave him all the money I could, but I had my mother, brother, and sisters to support. Within a year he was dead of shame and his wife and unmarried daughters were selling themselves to visiting traders. So I will tell you that there were times when I hovered close to the prince not to save him from going over the ramparts, but to push him. His total innocence in both deed and knowledge merely made him doubly despicable in my eyes. Only the thought of my mother and sisters and my fear of mutilation—further mutilation—and death enabled me to forbear. Yet the prince would say, "Ah, Channa, loyal Channa, you are my only true friend on earth." What a pathetic creature he was!

One day in his twenty-ninth year, when his wife, the sad-eyed Yasodhara, was in the first agonies of childbirth, the prince was in a foul temper. "Why can't I see my own wife?" he kept shouting. "Why can't I see my son come into the world?" Several times he rushed down the hall to the princess's chambers, but his aunt, Prajapati, blocked his way. "What kind of a man are you?" she said. "Whoever heard of a man so worried about women's work! Yasodhara is of no use to you now anyway. Go off and amuse yourself with some pretty women, and when you return Yasodhara will be your slim beautiful wife again." The prince scoffed at her and walked off, but when he returned to his chambers he asked me to have his chariot brought around.

Whenever the prince wanted to go to the pleasure garden, I would inform the palace guard, who would ride well in advance to clear the way of all sights that might offend his innocence. I do not know how it happened, but as we raced down a long avenue of trees, I saw ahead of us, at the intersection of a country road, a crooked old man supporting himself with an equally crooked staff. I tried to distract the prince by drawing his attention to an utterly unremarkable rock formation on the opposite side of the road, but as we came near the old man he commanded me to halt. "What is this thing?" he asked with a look of horrified incredulity.

The old man was truly the most shrunken and wasted living creature I had ever seen. The dome of his skull was crossed only by a breath of white hairs. His eyes were clouded over with a whitish blue that gave a penetrating radiance to his blind gaze. He had no muscle at all, only a twig-like frame of bones on which his flesh hung like ancient yellowed silk, just a moment from turning to dust. The sigh of a sparrow could have knocked this man over, but somehow he had escaped the vigilance of the palace guard.

For a long moment I was too astounded to speak. Finally, only half aware of what I was saying, I answered, "This is an old man."

"But he is not just old. Look at him. His skin is melting."

This is the moment that changed my life forever. I had gathered my wits enough to know what I was doing. And I made a choice. And with that choice the prince and I entered into a bargain, though this was something I would only be aware of much later. "This is what happens when a man gets old. It happens to everyone—me, you, your excellent father—if we live long enough."

My tongue was in ecstasy speaking these simple and forbidden words. But a moment later the enormity of my transgression loomed over me like an executioner's axe. The prince sank onto his velvet couch and ordered me to head back to the palace. As I drove I sweated in dread that he would ask me to explain the secret behind the words, "if we live long enough." But he remained in silent consternation the whole way home. When we arrived he sent me to my alcove, and walked off in the direction of the stairs to the ramparts.

I didn't venture into his chambers until evening. He grabbed both my shoulders as I walked into the room and spun me around. "Sit down, my good Channa. Sit down here with me." He was smiling, all but laughing, as he dropped onto a heap of pillows. Bewildered, I lowered myself beside him.

"I want to thank you for what you told me this afternoon." He took my shoulders again. "You have changed my life. Everything has come clear to me now. Channa, you are a wonderful man. You are the great genius of this household. You are a buddha. I have always known it. And I do not deserve to have so excellent a man as you for my servant."

I was relieved to see him in such good spirits, but could not for the life of me understand how it had come to pass. I could only think that the sight of another's decrepitude had made him grateful for his youth and for the sublime comfort in which he lived.

The next morning, when the prince heard that Princess Yasodhara was still in labor, he looked at me strangely and said, "Well, there's nothing for us to do but head off to my pleasure garden once again."

When we came to the crossroads I was relieved to see that the old man was gone. The grass where he had been standing rose green and virginal, and seemed to have been touched by nothing heavier than the morning sun. The prince ordered me to stop. For a long time he looked down the rutted road and then told me, "Go here."

"But, your highness, the pleasure garden is this way."

"I don't want to go to the pleasure garden," he said almost regretfully. "If there is a road here, then it must lead someplace, and that is where I want to go." He patted me on the back and smiled. "I want to go someplace I have never been before."

This was when I became aware that the prince and I had made a bargain. In the twenty-one years that I had been in his service I had been almost as cut off from life as he had. True, I had had access to the servants' savory and sordid world, but I had only been off the palace grounds three times: to attend the funeral of my father and the marriages of my two sisters. The prince's words, "I want to go someplace I have never been before," unleashed a desire that had been contained so long I had hardly known it was there. "All right," I said and, repressing a smile very like his own, I yanked the reins and the horses pulled us around.

The road descended steeply along the edge of a cliff into a deep river valley, and was so narrow that several times our wheels came within a hand's breadth of spinning out over emptiness. But it was not long before we reached the valley floor and were riding beside a high clay bluff, splattered from its base to its crest with small round holes, in which we soon realized people were living. On a flat space in front of one of these holes a small crowd was gathered. These were poor people, dressed in rags, with naked, swollen-bellied children. They were yammering loudly in a dialect that I could only half make sense of. To the prince it was sheer gibberish. He told me to stop and leapt from the chariot before I had even drawn on the reins. He tripped on the uneven road edge and tumbled over his shoulders into a bush of thorns. When I got to his side he was already on his feet, his face streaked with small cuts and his eyes rolling with a wildness I had never seen in him before. He shoved me aside and strode up the dirt path.

Something was happening on the ground at the center of the crowd. A fight perhaps, two men rolling in the dust. Whatever it was so occupied the yammering observers that none of them noticed our approach until the prince was almost within arm's length of them. Then a woman shouted and, like swarming bees, the crowd instantly abandoned its original focus and regathered around the prince. I beat the filthy, stinking brown backs—men's and women's alike—and forced my way to its writhing, ravenous center, where the prince was being prodded, grabbed, and caressed by a hundred hands. He swayed helplessly, like a puppet, but in his face I saw the wild frenzy of the crowd magnified many times. "What do they want?" he shouted in my ear, when at last I was by his side.

"What else?" I said with disgust. "Money! Gold!"

"What for?"

I didn't have a chance to answer. The prodding hands swept us both up the hill to where a man lay writhing on the ground. His eyes were rolled up. His jaw was clenched ferociously. His scant yellow teeth tore the flesh of his gums, so that blood streamed from his mouth. It was impossible to say what age he was. His hair was perfectly black, but a fan of lines split his cheeks like shattered glass, and all the veins and muscles of his neck were as visible as if he'd had no flesh at all. One young woman, who might have been his wife or his daughter, knelt at his side and tore away the sweaty rags around his body to show us the great purple, rootlike swelling in his arm pit. She wanted money for his funeral. All of them were shouting, "Please! Give us gold to send this good man into the next life."

"Quick! We must get away from here!" I said to the prince, but he was gazing down at the dying man with stupefied fascination. I grabbed his arm. "Come, your majesty. It is not safe here." The prince, who seemed to have lost all will power, yielded to my grip and, knocking aside these feeble, filthy people, I got us back to the chariot. However, as I tried to draw him up beside me, he became as rigid as a rock.

"Give them gold," he told me. When I drew out only a few

pieces, he ripped my purse from my hands and threw it into the crowd.

We returned to the main avenue and, as I had expected, he commanded me to head back to the palace. Once again he was silent for most of the ride, but when we came to the crest of the hill just outside the gates of Kapilavastu and we could look across the whole green butterfly shape of the palace and its gardens, he asked me, "What has happened to that man?"

I had been expecting this question, but had been unable to prepare an answer. My tongue spoke for me without hesitation. "He is sick."

"Is this also something that happens to everyone?"

"Every man can become sick. You yourself have been sick many times." I told him what had actually been happening when winter and summer had seemed to pant simultaneously through his window or when his bowels had squirted yellow.

"Why didn't anyone tell me what was really the matter?" he asked.

I said nothing.

"That was a cruelty worse than the sickness itself."

I still said nothing.

"But I have never been like that man, have I?" he asked, a sudden desperation in his eyes and voice.

"No. You are strong and have led a good life. Perhaps you will never become sick like that." I thought this would comfort him, but instead he threw back his head and covered his face with both hands.

"I am a fool!" he cried. "I despise myself!" We did not exchange another word that day.

The truth is that I had never put much stock in Kondanna's prophecy. I had known too many so-called "seers" who were only cheap magicians and con artists. But also it was a matter of my temperament: The more passionately the majority of people believe in something, the more likely I am to doubt it. I have always been like that. But now that the prince had seen two signs just as Kondanna had described them, I was beginning to worry. That evening, as I lay on my bed wondering what I should do, a guard wrenched back the curtain of my alcove and dragged me into the hall. Although I accompanied him readily, he never loosened his numbing grip on my arm, nor replaced his drawn sword. He would not speak a word to me, but I soon gathered that I was being brought to the king.

"Dear Channa," his royal majesty murmured intimately as I knelt in front of him, "I am worried about Siddhartha. Twice he has set out with you for his pleasure garden and then changed his mind, returning to the palace in the most odd and irritable of moods. He gave me strange stares all last night and this morning he asked me why the skin around my eyes is crinkly, like a scrotum. Can you tell me if there is anything in particular that is bothering him?"

I answered, but I don't know what I said, probably something about the prince being anxious about the impending birth of his son and heir. My tongue rattled on and on and only subsided when I saw a grim resolve enter the king's expression. He indicated that I should stand, and when I had done so, he put his hands on my shoulders.

"You know, Channa," he said wearily. "I have always placed a great deal of trust in you. I hope that I have not been making a mistake."

I hardly slept that night. I made a hundred plans for escape from the palace and abandoned all of them. In the early morning, when the sky was still gray and the palace paving stones were still slick with dew, my curtain was wrenched back for the second time. It was the prince. He too looked as if he hadn't had a moment of sleep the whole night. His voice was breathy. I could hardly hear him. His blue eyes lolled deliriously.

"I have already summoned the chariot," he said. "We are going to my pleasure garden as soon as the team is harnessed."

There was nothing I could say to change his mind.

It was still early morning when we descended into the narrow valley, and a thick mist rose off the river and the perspiring trees. In places the mist would swirl into such a dense grayness that the road was obscured entirely and I had to rely upon the intelligence of the horses to keep us from spilling over the edge. When the road leveled out, the mist was so thick that daylight hardly penetrated it. Thus it was that we heard voices before we saw any people. The voices were united in a low deformed wailing. Although the prince had never heard such a sound, something in him knew what it meant, for it had hardly floated to us out of the fog than he fell backward onto his couch, cringing like a small child.

I drew the horses to a halt and told him we should go back. "It is dangerous here," I said. "There are evil spirits all about." I knew that at this moment I was being tested as a man and as a servant of the king. But when the prince said, "Go on. I want to meet these evil spirits," I gave the reins a feeble twitch and the horses pulled us forward into the fog.

We had only gone a few steps when I realized that a procession was about to cross our path. The horses stopped of their own accord. The flatness of the gray suddenly gained depth as a cluster of faint shadows moved within it. Gradually the shadows too gained dimension, becoming ragged clothing, gnarled limbs, and distorted faces. The members of the procession moaned, beat their breasts, and stumbled over the stony earth, but at their center, on a crudely carved wooden bier, the richly dressed corpse of the man we had seen in such agony yesterday drifted serenely through the mist, his eyes closed, cheeks smooth, and lips pressed gently together, as they might be just before a dreamy smile. He was astonishingly young, years younger than the prince or myself.

The prince, once again beside me at the reins, observed in a low, uneasy voice, "He has recovered from his illness."

"Yes," I answered.

"Then why are the people around him weeping and tearing their clothes?"

"Because he is dead." I don't know if the prince understood or was simply responding to the tone of my voice, but at my final word he flinched and a bewildered weakness came into his expression. I continued. I could not resist. "All of us are chained to a huge rock, a rock bigger than any stone in the palace, bigger than the palace itself, bigger than everything. And that rock is hanging over a cliff, moving down, forever, down and down. All our lives we are being dragged toward the edge of that cliff, every human being—you, me, your father— everyone without exception. And when we reach the edge, we go over. That is all. Everyone. Over the edge. Into death. Most of the time we try to forget what is happening. Sometimes we claw the sheer rock, trying to hold ourselves back, to escape the inevitable. But in the end we go over. And that is a truth your father has seen fit to have concealed from you your entire life."

As the last of the mourners filed in front of us, the prince was

silent. Then, softly, he asked, "What happens next . . . after
. . . after we . . .?"

I bit my tongue as it was about to confess the most terrible
secret of them all. The world was already pointless enough for
the prince. Were he to hear that the end of one life of dread and
confusion only meant the beginning of another, there would be
nothing that could stop him from casting aside all of his
privilege and fulfilling Kondanna's prophecy. So I told him a
different truth: "Nobody knows what happens after. Everybody's got their own idea and everybody is wrong. That's the
one thing you can be sure of."

I yanked the reins and turned the chariot back up the road
we had descended. The prince, sitting on his couch, lost in
thought, made no protest. When we arrived at the palace he
took me to his chambers. From a chest beside his bed he
withdrew a smaller chest and from this he removed two
blackened husks, which I soon realized were the petrified
cadavers of a rat and a tree frog. "Are these dead?" he asked.
I nodded. "I've been collecting these all my life," he said. "I
have found about twenty of them, but they never last very
long." Inside the box I saw a nest of small white bones and gray
flecks of desiccated flesh. "It has been very difficult to get them
into the palace without you or Vaharadas or anyone else
noticing." He drew the rat from my hands by its rigid tail and,
lifting it to his lips, inhaled deeply. He smiled and looked at
me. "You see, I too have kept secrets."

The following morning we were on the road again. This time
we did not turn at the road leading down into the valley, but
even so I had only the scantest hope that we would reach the
pleasure garden that day. And indeed the guards' sweep was
once more proven inadequate. About an hour beyond the
crossroads, near a boulder that sat like a huge egg in the high
grass, an ascetic in saffron rags appeared and extended his
cracked bowl toward the prince. There was an idiotic expression of blissful humility on his face. "Who is this man?" the
prince asked. I had already stopped. I did not have the strength
to resist the inevitable.

"A beggar," I answered.

"Why is he so happy?"

"Because he knows you are about to give him money."

The prince turned to the beggar. "What is your name?"

The man answered only by withdrawing his bowl and lowering his gaze to the ground.

"Does he understand?" the prince asked me. "Maybe you should speak to him. It seems to me that the people we have been meeting lately speak very strangely."

"His name is Vassavati." A young man, also in saffron rags, stepped from behind the boulder and swaggered toward us, apparently enjoying our surprise. "He used to trade in silver between Shravasti and Pataliputra. And, as you can imagine, he was often troubled by thieves, so often that he had a stout post hammered into the ground behind his shop so that he could personally bring the culprits to justice. One day, as a thief was being stripped and tied to the post, Vassavati lectured him about his evil ways and the rights of merchants and told him that he would be whipped until blood spurted from his eyes. But when it was time to take up the whip, Vassavati could not do it. He realized that every sin he had accused the thief of he had committed himself, many times over. How many people had he cheated in his travels up and down the Rapati? How many times had he maimed people merely for the crime of being poorer or weaker than he was? He had the thief cut loose, gave him the key to his shop, and vowed that he would never speak another word until he could speak the truth."

"He'll have a long wait," I said.

"It has been sixteen years."

"Who are you?" I asked.

The younger ascetic laughed. "I am nobody. Until he speaks and gives me a name I am only his tongue. I am his wagging tongue, cut out and rejected, licking the earth on which he walks."

I shouted to the horses, snapped the reins, and we were off at a gallop. The prince was furious. He wanted to talk to the young ascetic. He wanted to give both beggars every bit of gold in his purse. He commanded me to go back and I refused. No one had ever refused the prince's commands before, least of all me. He was astonished and infuriated and at a complete loss. I told him that the wisdom of holy men was just common sense stood on its head, and not worth the time it took to spit. I told him that what he had found out—what I had explained to him—over the last few days had completely changed our relationship. He had been lied to all his life, by everyone including his father, but I had blown the dust out of his ears. And now that he knew what a snakepit of pain and corruption he had been born into, he must also know that he needed a guide and a protector. For the first time in his life he could really be free, but only with my help.

I have said that I never wanted power and that is true, at least in the sense that I was not possessed by ferocious ambition as, for example, Vaharadas was. I am indolent at heart. I believe that I would have been perfectly content to have helped maintain the eternal springtime of the palace gardens for the whole of my days. But now I was fighting for my life. I knew that if I didn't take strong action against the unfolding of Kondanna's prediction, it would come true, and then my life would not be worth a roach's testicle. I wanted only to preserve my position, but to do that I had to change it utterly. Of course I had ambitions, but only those of an ordinary man—and perhaps that is why they came to nothing.

When we reached the pleasure garden, I had the laughing zebra women carry the prince to his chambers and there I had a pale giantess brought to him perfumed and naked, but he took no interest in her. He left his chambers by a window and strode across the Lawn of Whimsy, where a new troop of acrobats were performing: a whole village of bearded men and women—yes, the women also had beards!—who would stand on each other's shoulders, forming human towers so high that the uppermost member could grab the feet of soaring eagles and drop gently to the earth, dangling from the astonished, shrieking birds. But in these too he took no interest. He entered the Grove of Orderly Passion and climbed to the top of a rose-apple tree, where he threw another of his sulks, stopping the tree's shadow for most of the day. Only the arrival of a messenger announcing that Princess Yasodhara had borne him a son brought the prince down.

We returned to the palace at the head of a huge caravan of poets, singers, gymnasts, dancers, and clowns. The king had decided to honor the birth of his new heir, and to dispel his son's troubling moodiness, by holding the greatest celebration the palace had ever known. It was dusk when we arrived and the celebration was already under way. Chinese rockets shot over the city like the radiant ferns and gardenias of another, better world. Inside the gates, hovering over three bonfires, were towering silk balloons in the shapes of Princess Yasodhara, a plump pink infant, and the prince himself. All of them had the toothy grins of maniacs. When the prince caught sight of them, he buried his face in his sleeve. He had not said a word to me during the whole of our return journey, though twice he had taken hold of my hand and given it such a squeeze that I could feel the bones bend. As we advanced through the wild light toward the palace, the prince never once raised his head.

The Field of Heroes was filled with infants. From the palace itself to the outer ramparts, from the Lotus Garden to the Water Forest, there were nothing but downy heads and tender buttocks. In the great hall of the palace a hundred bare-breasted women on either side of the broad central aisle played on harps strung with their own hair. Cascades of milk spilled down the two side walls and flowed to a central pool where sleek, long-limbed children bathed and splashed. And finally, at the end of the hall, on a platform constructed entirely out of sculpted elephant tusks, stood two ebony thrones. On one of them sat the king and the other, empty, awaited the prince.

With a hanging head, the prince ascended a staircase composed of the bent backs of slaves and stepped into his father's embrace. The king looked at me over his son's shoulder with a gaze that was at once inquisitive and menacing. Only the absolute impossibility of escape kept me from bolting from the hall. I shrugged and mouthed above the cacophony: "Excess of joy." The inquisition in the king's gaze yielded to skepticism, but the menace remained. He turned his attention to his son and I took my place at the rear of the platform.

The king had arranged the most astonishing entertainments for the prince. From a land beyond the earth's spine, where the ground is always buried in snow and the trees and bushes are made of ice, he had brought a man who could reach deep into his own throat and turn his body inside out. There was also a magician who could make elephants dart in and out of the windows like starlings. And there were hundreds of beautiful, undulating dancers who had no bones and could twist themselves into any shape they chose. But the prince was numb to all of this. He never so much as lifted an eyebrow at the wonders that transpired in front of him. He drank heavily of the wine but didn't touch the mountains of rice, meat, and fruit that were heaped on every table. Finally, before the night was halfway to what would have been its crescendo, the prince fell asleep. The king tried to rouse him, but the prince only shrugged him off, saying he didn't want to move, he didn't want to do anything except be left alone. For a long while the king stared at his son, his face twisted with fury. But as the prince's inebriate snore blended once again with the din of the great hall, the king turned toward me and spoke in a low voice: "You have failed me, Channa. You have allowed Kondanna's lies to come true."

"No . . ." I threw myself flat onto the floor at his feet. "No . . . I . . ."

His sandaled foot struck my temple. "Silence, slug! I will eat your liver for breakfast."

"But he is not lost!" I protested. "I can still save him for you."

I don't believe the king heard a word I said. Letting out a bellow that silenced the entire hall, he leapt from the platform and vanished through a small door, but not without gesturing for the captain of the guard to follow him.

Without raising my belly from the smooth ivory, I scuttled over to the prince and clutched his ankles with both my arms, hoping that he would protect me when the guards came. Soon the courtiers, knowing full well the danger of remaining in the vicinity of a wrathful king, left the hall, and the performers, having no one but themselves to entertain, gave up their acts. For a long while the hall was filled only with a puzzled hubbub and the occasional crude laugh at a crude joke. But finally, being little more than barbarians, the performers began to partake of the massive quantities of food and drink abandoned on the tables. It was not long before a scene of the most atrocious debauchery ensued.

By dawn the guards still had not come for me. Except for a few couples copulating on the balconies, the entire hall was a tangle of unconscious bodies. Snores and groans rose like wisps of smoke over a leveled city. I had not closed my eyes once the whole night, but now, as the blue haze of the coming day was filtering through the windows, my eyelids grew intolerably heavy. I drifted in a state between dream and hallucination until a hand gripped my shoulder. It was the prince, who was sitting erect in his throne and seemed to have been awake for a very long time. "Loyal Channa, who has never lied to me," he said. "Can you tell me: Are all of these people dead?"

My heart was pounding and it was a moment before I had sense enough to speak. "No, Prince, they are only asleep."

"But they might as well be dead, isn't that so? They may not be dead now, but they all will be, sooner or later. So really there's no difference."

"Of course there is!" I was annoyed, at such a moment, to have to explain so obvious a fact. "When you're alive, you do things, you feel things. When you're dead, you don't."

"But what kind of difference is that!" The prince thrust himself from his throne. "Why feel things, why do things, if you are only going to die?"

"Because that is what life is." I too got to my feet. The prince was a child. He would be lost to Kondanna's prophecy through just this childish simplicity. "You're looking at it backward. Now that you know what you know, you should be happy. Don't you see how lucky you are? Aren't you glad you're not starving in some hole in the side of a hill? Why do you always see the dark side of things?"

"Good Channa." The prince stroked my cheek sadly.

"You still don't understand, do you?" I said. I had to be patient or I would lose him. This was my last chance. "You know the truth, but you don't really know it. Believe me, Prince, you're the luckiest man on earth. You'll find out soon enough. You're a new man now. You'll be astounded by how differently you'll see things. It'll be a new world, I promise you. Even with death . . . After a while you'll find it's not so difficult to live with death."

The prince stared silently across the hall for a long moment. When his gaze turned back to me, there was a hardness in it I had never seen before. He leapt from the platform and, stepping between the sleeping bodies, left the hall. I ran after him knowing that it was all over: I was lost. At the bottom of the great staircase he told me to saddle Kanthaka, his favorite horse, and bring her around to the courtyard outside Princess Yasodhara's chambers. I got down on my knees.

"Your majesty! You can't leave me behind!"

He shook his head and smiled. "Of course not." He took

hold of my shoulders and lifted me to my feet. "You are coming with me, at least part of the way."

The prince turned and vanished. For a long while I remained as if paralyzed at the bottom of the stairs. Only the fear of being spotted by the palace guard caused me to withdraw into a dark passageway. I soon found that the entire city had been as debauched as the great hall. Every third doorway sheltered a slumbering body or two. The streets were pungent with vomit and urine. Apparently the revelry of our proud citizens had progressed to such a point during the night that even the king's anger had not diminished it.

By a miracle, I managed to lead Kanthaka and a sturdy gray mare to the princess's quarters without being observed. It was already full daylight. My robes were drenched with acrid sweat. As I dismounted, my knees gave way and I thought I was going to faint. The prince stepped out of a doorway with a bag over his shoulder. I reached to take it from him, but he shook his head. We mounted and made our way silently through the unconscious city. At the gates there were three smoldering heaps of ash. The two larger balloons lay flat on the ground, but the smallest, the infant, had settled on the fire. Only a scorched pink arm remained. There were no guards. The gates were ajar. As we passed through them onto the open road, my pulse quickened for the first time with the hope that I might survive.

At the crest of the hill the prince stopped his horse and looked back at the yellow clutter of the city and the spired palace with its wings of spring green. "I wanted to see my son at least once before I left," he said. "But he was asleep in Yasodhara's arms and her hand was over his face. I was going to move the hand, but then I became afraid that she would wake up and keep me from going . . ." He fell silent, tugged his horse around, and we moved off down the long avenue overarched with trees that we had taken so often to his pleasure garden. After a while he spoke again. "When I have found what I am going to seek, I will come back. And I will see him then."

I wanted to say, "What is there to seek? You are going to find nothing. There's nothing out there any better than what you're leaving behind." But I said nothing. I had to stay in his good graces. What was I without the prince? A man who belonged to neither one caste nor the other, a man who was not a man and not a woman. Even if I were to escape the king's wrath, what future would I have? I saw myself wading up to my neck and then over my head in a bog of blood and excrement, in this cessmire of a life.

When we had crossed the Anoma River, which marked the southernmost extreme of his father's kingdom, I saw what the prince's bag contained: two things only, a cracked bowl from the kitchen and a length of rough saffron-colored cotton cloth. I have told you that I am a weak man, and I am. Here was my last chance to avert the fulfillment of the prophecy, but I did nothing. I wanted to cry, but I kept silent. I did as I was told. The prince was ludicrous. He was a fool. With his dull sword he hacked away at his beautiful blue-black hair, making gouges in his skull, pulling whole hanks out by their roots. He took off his fine silk clothing and his jewelry and told me to put them on. I did. And he wrapped himself inexpertly in his rough cloth. I could see that it would fall off him at his third step, but I said nothing. Ludicrous! Ludicrous! There he stood half-naked, with his pale, tender feet hunched on the road's sharp stones, his head bleeding, and a fantastic excitement in his eyes. He kissed Kanthaka, told me to mount her and ride her back to the palace.

I could hardly speak, with the absurdity of it, with my rage. My voice was like the squeak of a well wheel. There were tears in my eyes. "But, Prince Siddhartha, how can I go back to the palace without you?"

"Just ride," he said, and laughed. I almost hit him with his own sword. He became serious, "Oh, Channa, my good friend, my only friend, I am sorry to be leaving you. I am sorry most of all because it is only my own stupidity that makes me leave. I must seem pathetic to you who have always known what I only hope to discover."

"What do I know? I don't know anything at all."

He smiled warmly. "Enough of that. You have always made too little of yourself. Go back to my father and tell him that I have made you my brother. Occupy my chambers. Take all of my possessions. You know so much better how to use them than I. Tell my father that I want you to be the tutor of my son."

Kanthaka was as reluctant to go as I, but the prince whispered similar rubbish in her ears and finally she turned and waded into the river. The gray mare followed of her own accord.

I never took up Kathaka's reins. After a while I even forgot that I was riding. My mind was as empty as a gourd and my will was utterly extinguished. I might have ridden all the way back to the palace—and to my death—had I not been set upon by thieves. They took Kanthaka and the mare, but left me the prince's clothes, which I sold for a pretty penny. I made my way south and eventually found work aboard a merchant ship. I have seen much of the world and have been to places that I would never have believed existed had I heard about them in the palace gardens. But it is to gardens I have returned. I surround my masters and mistresses with perpetual spring. It is the thing that I do best and enjoy most; not a deception, but a way of making peace with this earth.

The Only Life

I first met the fiendish Albert Zot many years ago when I we a young field agent for the Pest Control Commission making an extermination run along the Perimeter Wall. He was crouched on the rim of a frozen horse trough, slipping his skinny tongue through a crack in the ice, drinking. As soon as I spotted him I picked up a piece of broken broomstick and raised it over my head. I was pretty fast in those days, but the rats were generally faster. Every now and then, however, I would catch one so preoccupied with a piece of savory garbage that he wouldn't notice me, or I would trap one in a corner where he could only claw the wall and shriek. These were the moments when my job was most real to me.

While I was still a couple of yards away from Albert, my feet crunched on the crusty snow. He lifted his head and looked right at me. I was sure that I had lost him. But instead of running off, he turned completely about and watched me approach, looking me up and down, paying particular attention to my upraised broomstick. When I was within easy striking distance, he lay down along the rim and stretched his head out, so that I couldn't miss.

I had been a field agent for a good year now—ever since the

war ended—and had never seen a rat behave like this. I was so astonished that I just stood there with my broomstick up in the air. Finally I concluded that I had come upon a victim of my poison in the very last stage of his agony. I decided to watch. As I lowered the broomstick, I heard a tiny cry: "No! Do it!" I looked around to see who had spoken, then turned back to Albert, who had lifted his head. "Please. This is the way it should end." The words had emerged from his precise little V of a mouth—there was no denying it. "I'm waiting for you. Please." With a tiny, graceful movement that was startling in its resemblance to a human gesture, he lowered his head once more and stretched out his chin.

How could I kill this creature now? I dropped my broomstick and reached out for him. He looked ill: He was emaciated, his coat was tufty and dull. As I lifted his warm body off the cold concrete, I could feel his heart vibrating under the tip of my index finger. "No. Please . . . Please put me down. Just do what you were going to do."

"Why?" I asked. "Why do you want me to kill you?"

He didn't answer. I lifted him close to my face and saw not the slightest glimmer of more than rat-cunning in his stickpin eyes. For a moment I was embarrassed and slightly horrified that I had spoken to a rat. I was about to put him down again and leave when I felt him quivering. I lifted him once more and saw that he was sobbing. The fur beneath those stickpin eyes was dark with tears. I put him into one of my pockets and went home.

When I arrived, my mother was busy washing Quince, my infant son, in the bathroom sink. She told me that Anna, my wife, had already gone to work. I told her I'd forgotten my lunch. I hurried into the kitchen and put Albert, together with a bowl of water and some bread, in an old oil tin that I had been using as a wastebasket. Covering the top with a piece of masonite and a brick, I slid the tin behind the water heater in a closet off the kitchen, where I was fairly certain it wouldn't be found. Even so, all day long I worried that my mother or my wife might hear Albert scratching or, worse, talking, and pull open the closet door to investigate. When I returned home that evening, however, the only news was that my brother-in-law had promised to get us a radio from a friend in the black market. I didn't dare pull Albert out of his hiding place until later that night.

Anna fell asleep almost instantly, but I heard my mother turning pages on her bed in the living room for nearly an hour. When at last the quiet of the house was interrupted only by three rhythms of slumberous breathing, I took my overcoat from the back of the bedroom door, crept past my mother, and locked myself in the freezing kitchen. I had to fumble in the darkness behind the heater because I didn't dare turn on the light. Cold orange streetlight shone across the kitchen table. I removed the masonite and reached into the dark tin, expecting to be bitten. At first I thought he wasn't there, but then my fingers brushed his soft warm bulk in a corner and he rolled over, right into my hand. I placed him on the streetlit Formica directly in front of me. "Sorry about locking you up like that," I said.

"That's all right," he answered wearily. "I'm used to it." He pushed himself up onto his haunches, drew his knees up to the middle of his stomach, and rested his wirelike front paws on them. After a moment he heaved a tiny sigh, picked up his tail and began stroking it with an intensity that would have seemed manic in a human, but which in a rat seemed only ratlike.

For a long time I didn't know what to say. Finally I asked the question that had been on my mind all day: "Why did you want me to kill you?"

He answered by telling me who he was.

I was aghast. How many times had I, like half the world, cursed this monstrous administrator? How many times had I imagined myself at the head of a mob chasing Albert Zot down some alley, trapping him, tearing him limb from limb? And now, here he was on my kitchen table, a bony brown rat. I could have crushed him in an instant, with one hand! And perhaps I should have. But instead I talked, I asked questions. And Albert answered, reluctantly, but with a growing sense of relief. And from almost his first word I had the sense of being in the presence of a miracle. Albert Zot, the architect of the evil that had scorched half the earth, was possessed by a remorse beyond my comprehension.

That night we talked for a couple of hours, until Quince woke up crying for a feeding. I put Albert away hastily and brought Anna a bottle. It was the same the next night and the one after. I told Anna that I had insomnia and that sitting in the dark kitchen helped me relax. She accepted my explanation, more or less, but I knew that I would soon have to tell her about Albert, or get rid of him. On his part, Albert seemed perfectly content to spend most of his day in a tin behind the water heater. He hardly touched the food and water I left for him.

Albert had come to his remorse gradually. During the war, when his picture had been plastered on every corner, he had absolved himself by the rationalization that he was being made into a scapegoat, that many of his accusers had worked right by his side and so shared his guilt, and that, although it might appear otherwise to the ignorant and naive, he had not been operating with a free hand; he had been constrained by events, misled by his advisers and, in the final analysis, only following orders. "I didn't begin to question my innocence until I had been on the run for nearly a year," he told me. "I was still a man, but I was living like a rat: only traveling at night, eating out of garbage cans, and sleeping under the floorboards of people's houses. I had made myself a comfortable lair in a crawl space under the kitchen of a house occupied by a family of refugees from the north. The kitchen was really just a shack hitched to the back of an old stone house. At a couple of points there was just enough space between the walls for me to sit up and peer out at the family through chinks and knotholes. Whenever I wasn't out scavenging, I would sit there, hold my breath, and watch these miserable people.

"Every one of them had been horribly burned. They were missing most of their fingers and toes, their skin was raw and shiny, and only the scantiest wisps of hair waved around their skulls. I had seen many people like this before, of course, on the street and during the war, but I had never spent any length of time in close proximity to them. It wasn't so much their physical deformity that got to me. I had become used to that. It was the way their lives had been deformed, even the little things. The old man had no fingers at all. He couldn't scratch himself when he was itchy. He couldn't hold a spoon or a fork. The only way he could eat his daily gruel was by lifting the bowl to his face and lapping it out like a dog. All of them had problems like this, and much worse. Not a day went by when one of them didn't get the shakes, or wake up screaming from a nightmare. They kept being revisited by the fire. The young woman was the worst. She would have such fierce convulsions that they would all have to sit on her arms and legs to keep her from hurting herself. She was pregnant when I moved in. The baby was born shortly before I left. It was tiny, about as big as your hand. And it didn't cry, it squeaked. I saw it only once. It died after a few days.

"Living in the same house with these people, I stopped caring whether I was ultimately and perfectly responsible for what I had done. I could have been a completely passive instrument of fate, a mere conduit—it didn't matter. I had done what I had done. Without me these people never would have known such suffering. It was that simple.

"I had by this time already begun to think of myself as a rat. I was always saying to myself, 'you vermin,' 'you plague on humanity.' From there it was only a small step to the conclusion that I should *be* a rat. What I was really doing was facing the truth about myself. *I was a rat.* I had never been a man. So one night, several days after the baby died, I slipped out of my crawl space. I remember it was very cold. There was freezing rain. I took off all my clothes. Piled them neatly on the porch. And walked off into the rain, to begin the life I have lived ever since."

On the third or fourth night of our conversations we were discovered. I hadn't heard a thing, but in the middle of a sentence Albert sniffed, toppled sideways off the table, and scurried behind the root bin. Anna was standing in the open door behind me, hugging herself against the cold. "I heard voices," she said. "Who were you talking to?"

There were many ways I could have answered this question. Influenced perhaps by the conversation I had just been having, I decided to make a clean breast of it. Albert could not go on living under the sink forever, at least not without being discovered.

"Albert Zot," I answered plainly.

She thought I was joking, of course; and at two in the morning, when both of us had to be up in only a few hours, she was in no mood for a joke.

"No, I'm serious," I told her. "Look. Just wait a second. I'll show you." Albert had cornered himself. I reached the whole length of my arm behind the root bin and grabbed him around his soft and surprisingly elastic middle. When I drew him out, he dangled off either side of my hand like a wet sock. I think it took Anna several moments to realize exactly what I was holding.

"This is Albert Zot," I said. I lifted him so that his drooping muzzle was at my eye level. "Albert, I want you to meet my wife, Anna."

"A rat! Jesus Christ!" Anna had backed through the door and grabbed hold of the knob. "What did you bring that home for? Are you mad! What's gotten into you!"

"Anna, this is not a rat," I explained as calmly as I could. "Albert, say something. Tell her who you are."

"Get that thing out of here!" Anna shouted. "It's diseased! We've got a baby in this house, for Christ sakes!"

"Albert, just say hello. Anything. Please, Albert, speak." Albert remained mum and pathetically limp.

"What's going on here?" said my mother. She had come up behind Anna in the doorway.

"Your son has lost his mind!" said Anna. "He's brought a rat home from work!"

Just at that moment Quince began to cry for his midnight feeding.

"He what?" said my mother.

"Oh, Lord!" cried Anna. "Now Quince wants his bottle!" To me she said: "Would you get rid of that thing! I'm not coming in there until you've gotten rid of that rat. Take it out into the yard and throw it over the wall."

"I'll get you the bottle," I said.

"No! Don't you touch it! Don't you touch anything until you've gotten rid of that beast and washed your hands."

"Why did you bring home a rat?" my mother asked.

"He's not a rat," I answered feebly.

Hungry and neglected, Quince was rapidly lifting his cry to its most desperate and nerve-racking level.

"Just get out of the kitchen!" shouted Anna. "I want to get his bottle."

"I'll get the bottle," declared my mother, who was always eager to prove that she was more possessed of maternal virtue than her daughter-in-law.

Without a word Anna shoved her aside and retreated into the dark apartment. My mother edged gingerly into the kitchen, opened the ice box, and pulled out the bottle, eyeing the dangling Albert all the while. "It really is a rat," she observed incredulously. Then, adopting a conspiratorial tone, she continued: "Why did you want to frighten Anna with a thing like that? Really, take it outside and throw it over into the neighbor's yard. Let them deal with it."

"This isn't a rat. This is Albert Zot." I held him out toward my mother. "Come on, Albert, say something. Speak." But Albert was never to speak to anyone but me. As soon as my mother had fled, he looked up and said, "Why don't you do what they want? Really. It would be better."

In the morning, although I ceased to maintain that Albert was truly the fiendish Albert Zot, neither Anna nor my mother would grant me permission to keep him in the house. I wandered the streets with Albert in my pocket, trying to think of where I could keep him. He didn't want my protection. Many times he asked me to let him go. But I couldn't bear the idea of abandoning him once again to his life as a rat.

Partly it was the sheer magic of the thing: A talking rat in my pocket—how could I let it go? But also it was a matter of sympathy: During our nights of conversation, although he had spoken of his life as a man with nothing but scorn, I came to a new understanding of the Albert Zot I had hated as bitterly as any man or woman on earth. I saw how it was possible, through one comparatively innocuous step after another, to approach a tremendous atrocity. I saw how all of the things he actually did bore almost no tangible relation to their awful consequences. He was a man of words, after all, of rhetoric and ideas; not of action. It made me sick as I listened to him, actually dizzy, not because I thought I could do what he had done. I couldn't, of course, not now, not knowing what I do. But *then?* Before? If I had been him? If I had lived his life? Yes. I saw how it might be possible, merely possible, and that was enough to make my head reel.

But it was more than that. I also saw how his guilt had made him suffer. It had literally transformed him, after all. He was not the Albert Zot who had committed a crime against humanity. He was a pathetic and miserable creature. In his present condition I could feel nothing but sympathy for him. I know it is not an original idea, but I have come to the firm conviction that in a world where no one is perfect, forgiveness is the highest virtue.

I wandered the streets for more than an hour, dreading the moment when I would have to enter the doors of the Pest Control building. Thanks to Albert, I had developed a loathing for my work. Of course Albert was not, properly speaking, a rat, but even so, my sympathy for him had spilled over into his adopted species. I wanted to quit my job, but knew I couldn't. Times were very hard then and I was lucky to have a job at all. It was nearly nine and I was already in sight of the great, gray Pest Control building, when suddenly I was blessed by an inspiration.

With Albert still in my pocket, I walked into the building and went down to the basement, where I found a specimen cage, a water bottle, and a box of feed packets. I set up the cage right on the front of my desk, and then, on a large file card, I drew a picture of a sinister-looking rat face and wrote underneath in big block letters: THE ENEMY. Mounting the sign on the top of the cage, I took Albert out of my pocket and placed him inside.

My stratagem worked perfectly. The sign and, of course, Albert's name made his presence in the rat-extermination headquarters perfectly understandable. They also made it possible for most of my co-workers to give vent to their suppressed sympathy for the creatures they spent their days murdering. Albert was continually receiving gifts of peanut shells, bread crusts, and chunks of cheese. Hardly anyone could resist passing his cage without wrinkling up their noses, making kissing noises through their teeth, and saying, "How ya doin', Albie old boy?" There were, of course, sadists who poked at him with pencils and knives, or dangled mutilated rodents in front of his cage, snarling things like "Here's your dinner, Mr. Zot" or "Behold your fate!" But I made it very clear right from the first day that I was not going to allow any taunting or abuse of my pet, a stand that earned me a fair bit of taunting myself and the nickname "Ratman." But I didn't mind, and Albert never suffered more than a momentary nuisance.

Every morning when I went on poison distribution, I would take Albert along with me in my pocket. He would stand on his hind legs and push the pocket flap up with his head so that he could see. We would have long conversations. Sometimes my co-workers would hear me talking to him. It didn't matter. I would talk to him openly when I was back in the office doing my reports. But he would never answer unless we were alone.

I learned a lot about rat life from Albert, which increased my admiration for the species. They are immensely industrious creatures. A rat that isn't working as hard as it possibly can is dead. It is no wonder that they are one of the few species to have thrived since the war. We humans tend to see rats as a threat, as a symptom of decay, but I came to see them as a sign of hope, an inspiration.

I am sorry to say, however, that Albert also gave me information that enabled me to excel at my job. It was he, for instance, who told me about the ancient water main ("the Rat Riviera," as we came to call it) where, during any season of the year, the rodents of our city could have access to uncontaminated drinking water. He also told me about the "Rat Subways"—the two-hundred-year-old vacuum pipes that ran under all the downtown streets. The most important piece of information Albert ever gave me, however, was the recipe for a grain confection that no rat can resist and that, needless to say, has become an astonishingly effective medium for poison.

Albert never told me these things so that I could make use of them. They came up parenthetically, as details in the stories he told. I did my best not to let on to him how much the information he gave me contributed to the advancement of my career. But he was no fool. He heard people talking. He could see perfectly well that in a scant few months I had risen from lowly field agent to Deputy Commissioner of Pest Control. I'm sure he drew his own conclusions.

We only came close to talking about it once. I had been Deputy Commissioner for a year and had just been given the preliminary results of a study showing that during my tenure the ratio of rats to humans in our city had declined from three to one to an even one to one. I fully intended to give this study the widest possible publicity (I had, after all, learned more from Albert than just how to control the rat population), and this meant that I would frequently be discussing it in Albert's presence. So when I was done reading, I pushed the typed pages across my desk to where Albert was rocking back and forth on my blotter—one of his favorite ways of amusing himself while I was working. "Albert, I want your opinion of this."

I had never asked for his advice about my work before.

Intrigued, but also a bit frightened, he jumped down from the blotter and scuttled across the report. Rats do not have very good vision. The only way he could read was to walk along each line of text, appearing to sniff every word as he passed it. When he had gone back and forth across the report several times and finally reached the crucial statistic, he sat up, grabbed his tail with his two front paws, and said, "I'm sorry. I've had it up to here with official prose." He drew his paw in a slicing motion across his neck. "I'm afraid I can't help you." Dropping his tail, he began to lick his paws and stroke the fur on his snout and head.

"Forgive me, Albert," I said. "I just want to know how you feel about sharing an office with the man who has exterminated two-thirds of your species."

Albert clamped his tiny black eyes shut and pulled on his whiskers. Without a word or a glance, he dove off the table, scurried across the floor, and disappeared behind the bookcase. About an hour later I felt a tugging on my pants cuff and then the familiar prickle of tiny claws. Albert clambered into my lap and leapt onto my desk. I thought he looked distraught, although to be honest, after all this time I still had a great deal of difficulty reading his emotions. Taking a seat on my inkwell, he began to speak rapidly, as if he had rehearsed his speech many times and wanted to get it out before he lost his nerve.

"Please excuse my behavior," he began. "As you no doubt understand, you have touched upon a very sensitive issue for me, one to which I have given a great deal of consideration recently. I want to tell you the ugly truth: I have lived as a rat. I have made love to rats—although that term is perhaps a bit grandiose for such indifferent encounters—my only progeny are rats, but. . . *I am not a rat.* That is a fact and I hope it is not an evasion. You claim to admire them, but I find them a cold, conniving species. There is no love among rats, no loyalty, no sense of beauty. There is only hunger, anger, and fear. There. I've said it. I don't want to talk anymore."

I am afraid that I corrupted Albert Zot. When I first found him by the Perimeter Wall, he was crushed by shame, his existence only tolerable to him because it was one of unending hardship, humiliation, and pain. Had I not taken him into my care, I doubt that he would have lasted another week. Those first nights of confession revived him and so perhaps did my forgiveness—but only to a point. For a while he ate—never gluttonously, but regularly—and began to put on weight. But soon his despair gained sway over him again. He languished. He became indifferent to life. When I took him out on poison distribution, he would just lie at the bottom of my pocket. In his cage it was the same. The only way I could tell he was still alive was by the rise and fall of his belly.

After a couple of months, however, he began to change. It started with complaints. He would say, "Why do you keep me captive? Why don't you let me lead the only life I am good for?" I told him that he was too ill, that if I weren't there to feed him he wouldn't last a day. I told him that if he wanted to go when he felt better, he was free to. He protested, but not vehemently, and lapsed back into his indifference, but once more he began to gain weight.

One morning I came into my office and found him sitting up in his cage sniffing. My desk was near a partly open window. Outside it had just begun to rain. "I love the smell of rain on dry earth," he told me. I didn't answer because one of my co-workers had just walked into the office, but I noted with secret satisfaction that this was anything but indifference to life.

Then finally, one afternoon shortly after I had been made Deputy and moved to a private office, I was sitting at my typewriter finishing up a report, when I noticed him positioning himself on the edge of my desk with his back to the empty air. In the next instant he'd kicked his hind legs up over his head and landed with a gentle thump on my rug. A moment later he was back on my desk, his snout dipping toward the ground in a gesture that I had come to recognize as expressing rat embarrassment. He explained that as a young man he had won several gold medals in international diving competitions and that recently, as a way of passing his long nights alone, he had begun experimenting to see if he could adapt his old skill to his new circumstances.

By this time Albert was a robust example of *rattus norvegicus* and more than capable of leading "the only life he was good for," a fact that neither of us ever got around to mentioning. I don't believe that Albert had in any way forgiven himself or was trying to evade his guilt. Rather I think that, over time and in the pleasant circumstances that I provided for him, his guilt had become increasingly intellectual, more a conviction than an emotion. This is not to say that Albert didn't remain a profoundly morose creature, only that now his despair was not so much over his past sins as his present inability to live up to the ideal of his shame. Now when he turned down food it was not because he had no appetite but because he wanted to have no appetite.

Albert's inability to live up to his own ideal eventually affected me much the way it did him. I came to see that by attempting to preserve something miraculous I had destroyed it. I was no longer granting forgiveness to a creature martyred by transcendent remorse, I was supporting a whining, neurotic rodent, who was also a *criminal*—a fact I had always found hard to grasp. I began to dwell increasingly upon Albert's crimes, and to think that, although no punishment could ever reduce the evil he had done by so much as a jot, it was still not right that he continued to live in comfort and peace, that he was allowed the luxury of despairing over his own sincerity.

I grew to hate Albert's endless, tiny sighs and the clicking of his pink jaws as he sucked from his water bottle. "Be quiet!" I would shout at him. "Can't you see that I'm working!" There were moments when I became drunk with the enormity of my power over him. I would slap my open hand down on the desk, giving him such a start that he would do a complete flip in the air and land with his claws clutching and his pointy snout twitching. I would throw things at his cage. Several times I swept him off my desk or threw him across the room. People began to notice. My shouts were audible from the hall. Once or twice, after catching me in minor acts of sadism, my secretary said, "Why don't you get rid of the horrible thing?" But then I would feel a clutching in my chest and a warm prickle in my eyes, and I would remember how much I loved Albert's gentle weight resting on my shoulder or thigh.

The day the Director General called me into his office and told me that I was to be appointed Commissioner of Pest Control, I knew what I had to do. It was one thing for a Deputy Commissioner to have a pet rat, but the Commissioner, a purer embodiment of the civic will, had to be above that sort of humor. I acted quickly, without allowing myself time to think. On the way back from the Director General's office, I stopped by the basement and got a package of poisoned feed, the very confection for which Albert had provided the recipe. He watched eagerly as I let the pellets clink into his dish. I had been a bit neglectful about feeding him of late and no doubt he was exceedingly hungry.

Before eating, however, he looked up at me and said, "I hear you've gotten a promotion." His voice was somber, cautious. He had grown wary of my moods.

"Yes," I said, equally somber. "How do you know?"

He jerked his snout toward the door. "I hear people talking."

"Aren't you hungry?" I said.

"Starved. But I was just thinking . . . It seems to me that now is the time . . . I mean, now that you'll be . . ."

"I don't have time to talk, Albert. I've got to get a memo out tonight."

"All right," he said, seeming as eager to avoid the discussion as I. "We'll talk later, then."

"Fine," I said. I went to my desk and put a sheet of paper in my typewriter.

He ate rapidly and took a long drink of water, then lay down for a postprandial nap. I filled a whole page with nonsense syllables. Again and again I reminded myself that he was the murderer of millions.

It wasn't long before I heard a hiss of indrawn breath, a squeak, and then a frantic clatter of tiny nails against steel bars. I didn't lift my head until the clatter had subsided—less than a minute later. Albert was lying half on his back, looking straight out at me. His stomach was heaving visibly and his limbs had already begun to shiver. He knew exactly what I had done. He looked shocked, but I detected no reproach, no sense of betrayal. And I even thought, at the very end, that he looked relieved, but that may only have been the spark going out in his stickpin eyes.

Lost Goodness

I am the slave of the man who was my slave. I have known many things in my life, all of them wrong. But I am a different man now and the thing I know is that every man is a slave. But I hope I am wrong.

My master has a taste for tongue fruit.

My master is as weak as a woman's mustache.

My master came out of the sea.

The white sea poured like a river from his lips. Spray blew from his nostrils. Seaweed was his hair. Wilted roses were his clothes. This was in my former land, before I knew I was a master or a slave. I too was standing on the beach. My fish traps were whirling around my head. My fish traps fell into the sand. As my master rose out of the white, he made the ugliest noises of your tongue. He did not know I was standing there. He rose, the sea hissing off him, and his eyes rose and he saw me. Then he fell back down onto his knees and begged me not to eat him. I know this now because we have talked about it many times, but then I knew nothing.

I knew the sweetness of my mother's milk and my father's soft eyes.

I knew how to clamber the spiky tongue fruit tree.

I knew that ghost-men loved the clouds on top of Aulko.

And that dead-men loved the sea.

I knew nothing.

I know nothing still.

Death had opened its salt mouth and there stood my master. Blood was on his tongue. His eyes were green and they floated in blood. But his hand on my hand was a child's hand. And then I knew he was a dead-man asking me how to be alive. And I held out the long pink fruit of the tongue fruit tree. But he took it for the thing for which it is named and hit the wet sand with his face, making the most awful sound of the lonely dead. Eat, I said, and happiness will be in you. I lifted his face with my foot. I wrapped my fingers in his hair of seaweed and pressed the fruit on his mouth. And I never heard such a noise from a man's mouth. And never saw a man run like a snake. The white mouth of the blue sea opened to take him back and he spun and waved his arms like a lover of the sea. I spat and flung down his hair. I had no patience with the dead.

The dead can see only when the day eye is closed and the night eye is closed.

The dead don't eat.

The dead don't sniff the juices of love.

They make themselves into stones.

And sink into the sea.

Babies know more than dead-men.

I flung his hair back to the whiteness and picked up my fish traps. This night I would not eat fish meat.

My master will be a ghost-man.

No longer do I hate dead-men.

He did not sink like a stone. He was a bird who flies in the water. I saw him, a darkness in the blue, a shining, waving his arms. And then the whiteness divided and spilled down both sides of him. And on his hands and knees he crawled back across the sand to my feet. This was when I saw the foolishness of the wise mother and the wise father. I sent my wife to tell them a man had been eaten by the mouth of the sea and was not a dead-man. They came bearing the dull tongue fruit knives. The wise father sucked from the wise mother's full breast and spat on her withered one. Together they said:

The eyes of the dead are like two stones sinking into their deadness.

This man is watching.

The bodies of the dead are like spit in the fire.

The curses of the dead are like smoke in the black night.

This man is watching.

This man is not dead.

What is this man? I asked.

This is not a man, they said.

This man is a snake-man.

I did not have the hunger to tell the wise father and the wise mother that they were fools, or I would have said that I had seen this man walking on two legs. This man is a snake-man, all the people of my former land told each other. This man is a snake-man, they repeated like the tongue fruit slapping together in the wind. They began to gather wood for a snake fire. This man, my master, who would not be a dead-man, had crawled out of the sea to his death.

Get the snake knives! cried the wise mother.

The wise father began to sing the song of the snake feast. My master's mouth was eating sand, making the noises of your tongue. I lifted his face with my foot. I wrapped my fingers in his hair of seaweed and brushed the tongue fruit over his lips. He bit and swallowed. I lifted his hair until his head was next to my own. He was eating. I know this man is a man who wants not to be dead, I said. I knew nothing. The wise father stopped singing. The wise mother said, This man is a snake-man. My master was eating. The boy ran up with the snake knives but dropped them on his own feet. Thereafter people would point to the boy's feet and say, Those are the scars of the man-snake. Thereafter I was known as the man-snake's master.

My master the man-snake was good for nothing. His nose bled. There was the noise of the sea inside him when he breathed. He could not harvest the finger beans. He could not kill the blind pigs. There were times when I thought he was still dead. But he could eat. Even then I knew he would become a ghost-man. He had only one thing from his land, this land, your land. A piece of wood with a belly of shiny steel. And with this on his mouth he would play all your sad music. He told me all about your land and I felt myself growing with

knowledge. I knew your trees were stone and your birds were
steel and your birds sang the sad songs he played for me. I
knew that you ate your babies and murdered people for being
good. I knew there was no day eye in your land because men
had put it in boxes and made people pay with their blood for a
little sight to help them find their way through the always-
night. I knew nothing, of course. He told me how he crossed
the sea on an island of wood and how the men on this island
had thrown him into the sea. But he didn't say why. He told
me how he came to my land by flying through the sea like a
bird. Those were the words he used because there are not
words to say the thing that he did.

My master the man-snake had a taste for tongue fruit. My
master the man-snake was lower than a dog in the eyes of my
people. My people said I should tie him to a tree until his
hunger made him work. The wise father would sing the song
of the snake feast when he saw him. The wise mother would
spit over his shoulder. But my sister liked him and sometimes
would let him suck at her breast for all the night.

Then came the time when the tongue fruit trees shouted
curses.

Then came the time when the night eye wept fire onto our
roofs.

Then came the time when babies were born with beaks for
lips and every woman's breast went dry.

Boys ran through the streets crowing.

Wives woke in the night to find their young husbands
wrinkled and toothless.

Girls walked from house to house without talking, then they
cried from the clouds on Aulko. They had become ghost-men.

When the day eye had closed six times, half my people were
gone.

Then one day in the warm season it was snowing. And where
the sea touched the sky there was a shadow and above the
shadow the clouds hung limply, like the withered breasts of
our women. And out of the sea walked a whole village of men
with clothes like wilted rose petals and seaweed for hair and
some of them carried steel torches and some of them carried
huge knives that were not for the tongue fruit or finger beans,

but might have been for the blind pigs. The wise father stepped forward and made the greeting of the tongue fruit knife. Under the sky there was thunder and the wise father was lying in the sand. His body was falling to pieces. His blood mixed with the sand until the whiteness came and took it away. The wise mother screamed with the voice of a ghost-man before a huge knife cast her head into the mouth of the sea.

My people's feet splashed the sand.

My people's mouths were all open.

Their hair flapped behind their heads.

First my master stayed in one place. Then he walked toward the men who came out of the sea, speaking the noises of your tongue.

More shadows appeared between the sea and the sky. More men walked out of the sea. As the men of my people screamed out their death or made the silence of enslavement, I saw them curse my master the man-snake with their eyes. As the women of my people screamed out their death or made their false laughs, I saw them curse my master the man-snake with their eyes. I did not curse him because I saw in his eyes the great sadness of a child still bloody from the womb. I knew that he would become a ghost-man. The tongue fruit trees were silent.

As we crossed the sea on an island of wood, my master told me many times how he had wanted to save my wife and my sister and my son and my daughter.

He said, The master of all men told me one slave was enough for a valueless seed like myself. That one slave would have been your sister. I want you to know this. I do not want you to think anything about me that is not true. I wanted your sister, but so did the master of all men. So I chose you.

Thank you, I told him.

Do not thank me, he said. I am a valueless seed. You are the better man. You are better than all the men where we are going. That is why I saved you.

As the island of wood journeyed up the river to join the land it loved, I saw how happy the people of your land must be to have made so many children. From the rocks and from the river trees on every side of me yellow-skinned boys and girls leapt

into the green water. They have no fear of death! I thought.
Again and again they leapt into the water and clambered back
onto the rocks and the river trees like yellow monkeys. Never
had I seen children leaping into the mouth of death. How brave
these people are, I thought. Even their babies paddle on the
very lip of death.

Of course I knew nothing.

I know nothing still.

And your city, this city, was like the roar of the very throat of
death, only it never paused to take its salt breath. I was afraid
as I stepped from the island to your land, and took the bravery
of your children to teach me. I leapt to the land and it lifted
beneath my feet like the sea. I heard the moans of the monsters
you have made to serve you. I saw their huge eyes that reflect
the whole world. I saw people flying through the air. Tiny
women who could lift whole mountains onto their backs! I
heard music—the sad, sad music of your people—everywhere!
And such fruit! I had never seen so many kinds of fruit. Red
and orange and green and purple. Round and long and small
as a testicle and huge as a fat man's belly. But no tongue fruit.
And this made me sad, but it also made me hunger to taste the
fruit that could feed so many people without making them sad
that they were not eating the tongue fruit. None of these
people had the tongue fruit hunger, which is so common in my
former land, as common as the tongue fruit itself. I will learn
from these people. I will grow big with their knowledge, as big
as the mountains they live in.

I saw a pig made of jewels.

I saw a man breathe fire out of one nostril and water out of
the other.

I knocked the air and it broke to pieces.

The air was as warm as my mother's breath.

My master said, I'm sorry I brought you here.

I asked him why. I saw the great sadness of the newly born
in his eyes.

Look around you, he said. This place is evil. Everyone here
is suffering. You will be destroyed here, just as everyone is
destroyed. This place will kill you.

This is when I realized that my master knew nothing, even
about his home. I said, the day eye looks down for all to see.

No one has put it in a box. But my master said nothing. In his eye was the love of the ghostly world. Ghostly voices were in his ear. He did not hear me until I said, There is no tongue fruit here.

No, my friend, he said, taking my arm, there is nothing here as wonderful as the tongue fruit.

I ate your hard fruit and my heart turned to water and spilled out of me. Now I have a new heart and I eat your fruit all day long. It will make me strong.

My master has a wife and a daughter and a brother. He told me nothing of them in my former land and on the island of wood and on the long paths of your stony land. He told me nothing until he opened the door of his blue house, and Betsie, making the awful noises of your tongue, ran from us the way monkeys run from ghost-men. Your hard-footed people came from every side like hunters around a blind pig. Their eyes were wilder than babies' eyes. They formed a ring around my master and stamped the earth and cried like night doves, crazy with their loneliness, dancing the dance of lost goodness. And like piglets they leapt on my master and suckled from his cheeks, his mouth, his eyes. I went into a dark place to hide and then they were all gone. And then I heard my master come looking for me, making the loud noises of your tongue. And even though I heard his happiness, I was afraid. Making the loud noises of your tongue, my master brought me to where his people were sitting and they looked at me as if they were looking at a ghost-man. And my master made my name into a noise of your people. With the tongue of my people, my former people, my tongue, he told me, This is my wife, my daughter, my brother.

I saw the boxes where you put the day eye to see with and cook your food. I saw that you have made the air hard to let in the sight of the day eye and keep out the wind and show you at night when you are afraid that there is nothing outside in the darkness but your room and yourselves. I saw many wonders in those days and the loneliness of my mouth to eat with my people was forgotten by the many, many thoughts that were coming into my head. My master had happiness then, more happiness than I had ever seen in him, except in my land when he made the sad, sad music of your people. And slowly the words of your tongue were added to my words and I too had happiness. And I had a room near where the food was cooked until one day I saw that Betsie had nipples pinker than a baby's tongue. Then I was told to sleep on the ground. This is when I began to know that I know nothing. I slept on the ground with your strong beasts and scrubbed their hard sides and learned to love their shiny eyes that see everything. Thoughts spilled through my head and I never tasted loneliness.

My master is becoming a ghost-man.
My master has a taste for lost goodness.
He eats the fruit of your land but they are like air to him.
My master is good for nothing.

My master's sadness began at the gatherings of your people where you cover yourselves in many, many cloths that are fire and water made into one beautiful thing.
Where your people never stop laughing.
Where your people never stop moving like the tongue fruit free on a windy night.
Where your people drink happiness from bubbles on their hands.
My master drank happiness and it made him sad.
I too was covered in water-fire and brighter than the brightness of the day eye. I stayed out with the strong beasts and kept them peaceful. But always there were people around me. And always there were women. Your yellow women. And they would bring me inside and ask me to dance to your sad, sad music and they would laugh when I did the dance of the monkey in the thunder. And I would laugh. And they would ask me questions and they would laugh at the funny noises my tongue made of your tongue. When my master heard them he would tell them they were all blind pigs. He would tell them that I showed him how to live. He would tell them that they were rust and I was steel. I am the song of the day and they are the farts of dogs.
Now we do not go to the gatherings of your people.
Now I am not covered in water-fire.
At home my master sucked only sadness from the breasts of his wife. I brought her milk and she asked me to bring her wine,

not with anger in her voice, but with thirst. It was my master
who had anger in his voice and so much loudness that his
daughter's eyes leaked the salt blood of the dead. His wife's
eyes did not hear him. When he told his wife to bring the wine,
she left. He told me to sit where his wife had been sitting, and
when she came back with the wine he told her to serve it to me.
In that moment he died in her eyes. She put the bottle in his
hand and left. My master served me the wine.

My master's wife lives with a ghost-husband. He does not see
her when she is in the room. He does not hear her when she
speaks. And he does not speak to her, but he speaks to me.
And she does not see him, but she does see me. And her eyes
say, You have killed my husband.

I sleep in my master's bed and he sleeps on the ground beside
the beasts. He brings me birds brown from their juices and lost
in forests of spice. My master eats only what the rats eat. He
brings me wine and bows as he leaves the room.
    Why do you do this? I asked him. You are as thin as air.
    He told me that this bird was cooked over the fires of my
burning land. And that the blood of my people ran in rivers so
that his people could have this wine. I do not want to drink this
bloody drink, he said. Or eat this bird that stinks of murder.
    But the bird smells only of spice and tastes as sweet as the
milk of a new mother. And the wine fills me with the happiness
of a thousand red evenings.
    Good. If anyone should grow strong from this food, it is you.
For me it is nothing but evil.
    My master is good for nothing. He is a fire of wet grass. I
said, What is good is good. If it is good for me, it is good for
you.
    I did not say it is good for you. It is nothing but evil. It is the
flesh of evil and as we eat it we grow strong but evil grows
stronger. Our hunger for evil's flesh makes us its slaves, and
the stronger we grow the weaker we are beside it. Evil satisfies
its hunger by satisfying ours.
    My master is a bowl with a hole in it. My master is a man's
nipple. I said nothing.
    He said, Many times I have thought it would have been
better to have left you in your land and many times I have

thought I should kill you myself, before all the good in you is made to serve evil. But then I thought that it is only because there is evil that I would do this thing. And I thought that any time I do something because of evil I am the slave of evil. But of the many things I can do and will do, there is only one thing I can do if I will not be the slave of evil—I can do nothing.

My master ate the dirt I walked on.
He drank the sweat off my neck.
He wove his clothes of spider strings.
He became so empty that his skin fell between his bones.
He met the silence of his wife with silence.
His brother spat over my shoulder. At night I heard him sharpening the snake knives and singing the song of the snake feast.
Betsie told me: When your master dies they will kill you and I will be glad.

All of the things I was feeling became a monkey inside my chest and day and night the monkey banged on my bones and moaned with the crazy sadness of monkeys: Oh, please do something! Do something, please! I told Betsie that my master had sent me to look for the tongue fruit. I told my master's wife that only by eating the tongue fruit could a dead-man come back to life and a ghost-man grow strong. I walked the long paths of your busy land and saw that the eyes of your people gleamed like snake knives when they saw me. As I came toward them I saw in their eyes the joy-anger that makes parents want to mix the blood of their children with the blood of snakes on the night of the snake feast. I told them I had been sent by my master and hurried past before they asked me what he had sent me for. And I wished that he *would* send me. If only my master would be my master, then I could walk your long paths for a reason. If only he would suck the milk of life and grow strong, then this land would be my land and I would be free.

I told my master that only as fruit and flesh passed between his lips would they pass between mine. When he would not eat, I would not eat. When he spat his food onto the dirt, I would spit my food onto the dirt. He told me he could not stand to see his not-hunger sucking the flesh off my bones. He spoke in my tongue. Now he never used his own. In his tongue, your tongue, I told him, Eat and happiness will be in you and in me. He ate and I grew strong but he only grew thinner. Now he is as thin as a handful of weeds. Soon the sight of the day eye will weigh heavier on my back than he does.

In my land, my former land, my master had learned to speak with my tongue, but not with my eyes. He spoke of the tongue fruit as if it were more than a fruit. He spoke of my land the way mothers and fathers speak of the children they have killed in the snake dance. When he spoke of my land, I told him he knew nothing. I told him why the tongue fruit is red. I told him the true meaning of the song of the snake feast. I told him of the redness of my own hands on the night of the snake feast. My master said nothing. When I ate, he did not eat. When I put tender flesh to his lips, they remained closed like a healed wound.

I know there is evil in this life.
But my master knows better.
He knows nothing else.
He knows nothing.

When my master had grown as thin as a leaf, I carried him on my back when I went for my walks. He didn't want to go, but how can a leaf fight the wind? By falling, say the wise old men. And now I understand their wisdom. Like the wind I carried him down the long paths of your land.
    I showed him the mountain with the eye on its peak.
    I showed him the tree whose branches were lightning and whose leaves were clouds.
    The field where women tossed balls of dough into the air and warm, golden loaves fell back into their hands.
    He told me he was hungry for tongue fruit.
    I showed him the man made out of insects.
    The singing rocks.
    The huge stone knee.
    I showed him the house where boys ate meals off girls' bellies.
    He told me he was hungry for tongue fruit.

I told him tongue fruit is only good because we eat it.

He showed me a man of my people being led through your city with a ring through his lip.

I showed him the pig of jewels.

I showed him the tower of faces.

Everywhere I saw wonders, he saw evil. Everything that filled me with joy filled him with shame. When the tiny eyes of the night came down to the earth, even the weight of my master, which was less than a shadow, was more than I could carry. I lay down on your hard, black land and my master lay beside me.

You are blind, he said.

I know, I said. I wanted only to sleep. I know nothing, I said. And I am the slave of your eyes.

Look, he said.

Another man of my former land was led past with a ring through his lip.

That is how they will treat you when I am gone, said my master, smiling.

Betsie said they will kill me, I said.

Yes, maybe they will kill you, he said and then laughed the laugh of joy-anger. But in the sight of the day eye he begged me to forgive him in a voice not louder than the wind in the leaves. I would not forgive him until he ate. Knowledge is only knowledge when it feeds you, I told my master. He knew nothing and grew thin as a thought.

In the coolness of the day eye's first sight of your land, I walked down to the river. Like a dead-man I looked out across the water and like a ghost-man I was lonely for what is not in my life and with the strength of my hunger I forgave my master, for I know what it is to be him. But I am not my master. I am what I am. And when he is not, I will be what I will be.

Things are what they are.

Things are what they are not.

If I were in my former land, would my son see his father when he looked at me? Would my wife show me the pale sides of her thighs? Would my mother hold up her breast to me? Would my father offer me the gift of the tongue fruit? When I looked at these people, would I see the people I know?

I don't know.

I am a man who doesn't know.

Perhaps all of my people have taken the salt breath. Perhaps when the day eye looks down on my former land, nothing hurries under its watchfulness but the blind pigs. And perhaps under the coldness of the night eye no creature speaks to the one it loves. There is only the valueless murmur of the tongue fruit trees. Or perhaps every night my wife whispers my name into the basket of her hands because I am not there to answer.

I don't know.

And I must grow strong on this knowledge.

If I am not to become nothing.

In my bones the monkey makes his crazy moan. My master is only a breath on the wind, but in a day or a minute he will grow too disgusted to take nourishment even from the air. Perhaps this very minute. And then I will have nothing for a master, nothing to send me out on your long paths, nothing to protect me from the joy-anger of your people. This morning I stood by the river and thought about the cruelfather-cruelmother who surrounds this land, all land, my former land with his hunger. I watched the yellow bodies of your children drop from high trees and rocks into the mouth of death. I saw how easily and happily they ran to where I stood beside the paddling babies on the very lip of death. As they leapt they laughed at this father who knows less than a baby and is more afraid. But I am learning from them. I am learning the foolishness of the wise mother and the wise father. I am learning that it is possible to fall to the bottom of the stomach of death and still live.

Saint Corentin and the Fish

A brown man, with fingers like sticks and a belly like an onion
bulb, is Saint Corentin.
Nothing between his heart and heaven, the good man has lost
his sandal.
On his knees, sandal in one hand, both feet bare, head under
the table, feeling in the dark.
He has a vision: The sandal by the lake, in the grass, like the
collapsed hull of an abandoned dinghy.
Bang.
The saint is sitting on the floor, rubbing his head.

The sandal is nowhere. Not in the grass by the lake. Gone.
Good Saint Corentin, hermit in the wilderness, throws his
remaining sandal to the center of the lake. This is a lesson:
You can do without.
This is another lesson: Saint Corentin, standing in the middle
of his hut, the newly found sandal in his hand.
He flings the sandal after its mate.

The good saint makes a vow to take nothing but acorns and water.

And for days thinks of nothing but honey, oozing and amber
   with bits of bee still in it, and of apples, fresh from a boiling
   vat, slipping out of their puckered skins, and of white fish
   flesh crumbling on the tongue, its odor rising through his
   palate into his nose.
Proof, thinks the saint, that he must hunger until hunger loses
   its hold, until he can choose to eat or not, just as God brings
   or withholds rain without consulting the farmer.
Good saint, who cannot, as he worships, help but feel shamed.

By the lake, in the grass, Corentin, come to contemplate God's
   creation, can't take his eyes from a fat brown fish.
Hovering in the shallows, stirring silky mud with its lower fins,
   troubling the saint's reflection with its upper.
"Little brother," asks the saint, "why have you come so close
   to the shore?"
The fish twitches, first to the left, then to the right.
"Little brother," says the saint, "you are in danger. Go back to
   the deep water where you belong."
The fish twitches.
A whisper in a saintly ear: "My beloved, go get your rod."
Brown man, belly like an onion bulb, retires to his hut to pray
   for the soul of the fish.

As the sun descends into the dark of the pines, the fish stirs
   the mud under a shower of fire, and in the morning,
   through the lens of the still water, the fish looms larger, and
   seems larger every day, and every night the saint thinks of
   a fish in a fire.
Thinks the saint: The Lord has sent this worthy creature to
   remind me how far I have to go.
The fish is a token of God's love.
And every evening, in his prayers, the saint remembers the
   fish.

Wretched Corentin, driven from his hut by the stink of his
   crime, flings a picked skeleton to the center of the lake.
Falls to his knees: "Forgive me, my Lord."

And into the shallows comes a skull and a cage of bones,
   twitching left, then right.
This is a lesson: Remember your weakness.
This is another lesson: The bony fins stirring up a fog of mud.
   And when the fog recedes: a fat brown fish, twitching.
A voice in a saintly ear: "My beloved, get your rod."

———————

Creature of bone and blood, subject to time and space, accident
   and mistake, to frailty and the desire of flesh for flesh.
Good saint, who cannot, as he contemplates God's perfect
   freedom, help but feel shamed.
Spends a day and a night on his knees.
And in the blue clarity of morning, retires to his hut and
   emerges with his rod, to accept the generous sacrifice of the
   fish, from this day forward.
Not a scourge but a gift.
Token of God's love.
Freedom from hunger.

———————

Breaker of wind, swatter of flies, belly like an onion bulb.
Corentin, nothing between his heart and heaven.
Forgive him.

IV

A Current in the Earth

A simple impulse to draw it all into his breast—

Sergeant Major George Bradley
                              on a small chair
with dragon's feet, sipping weak tea with lemon
in the drawing room of his mother's cousin,
the Honorable Judge Carter (Fort Bridger,

Wyoming, 1869), listened as Major John Wesley Powell,
whose right arm ended
                              midway down his pinned-up
sleeve, and his sturdy wife, Emma Dean Powell,
described their expedition to the summit of Pike's Peak,

she being the first woman to ascend that height.
"We could look across the tops of neighboring mountains,"
said Mrs. Powell, "our view only limited by the curvature
of the earth itself."
                              "I do believe that the Creator intends

such sights," said the Major, "as premonitions of the hereafter.
Indeed, eternity itself would seem short by comparison."

And the young sergeant major wanted nothing
                                        but to fling
himself out across such vastness, God's wide earth

and sky, the way better Christians long to enter Paradise,
to drown himself in it, and, at the same time, draw eternity
into the narrow cage of his ribs.
                              "I understand," said the Judge,
as the company was summoned to the dinner table,

"that you intend to make another expedition this summer?"
"No," said Mrs. Powell.
                        "Yes, indeed," said the Major,
taking hold of his wife's hand. "By boat this time, through
the last blank spot on the map, the canyons of the Green

and Grand rivers, from just a few miles east of here down
to northern Arizona." Sergeant Major George Bradley lowered
his cup to the floor and, standing along with the rest, his lips
chapped, his collar chafing, touched
                              Major John Wesley Powell

on the shoulder of his ruined arm . . .

———————

August 14, 1869
All night in the perfect darkness, with my cheek against my
soggy knee and the rain slapping my skull, dripping off my
ribs, I was haunted by that afternoon at Judge Carter's.
Moments or fragments of moments came back to me again and
again with extraordinary vividness. I heard all the words and
saw the faces: the Major's, Mrs. Powell's, even my own face, so
respectful and young. The only difference was that I was cut off
from myself, a mere observer, unable to speak or act, unable to
influence the events that transpired in front of my eyes, which
fact colored the whole experience with a certain sad fatalism. It
is not surprising, I suppose, that I should have been beset by
such dreams or memories this dismal night. Had it not been for
that sunny afternoon, I would not be here now, hunched
beside a plunging flesh-colored river at the bottom of a mile-
deep split in the earth's crust. Three months of hard traveling.

Nothing but rain for the last four days. Nothing to eat but moldy biscuits, dried apples (so called), and black coffee. Nothing ahead as far as we can see but this boat-wrecking, river-churning, jagged, black, unerodible granite. Not since taking a bit of shrapnel at Fredricksburg have I felt more in danger of dying. Yet here, amid these immensities of time and rock, there is nothing sordid about death. It does not seem a mistake, an awful waste, as it did when I glimpsed it briefly on the battlefield. And were I back in Judge Carter's drawing room, even knowing what I know now, that eternity is nothing like Paradise, I still would not hesitate to stop the Major at the door, as our company retired to the Judge's dinner table, and beg to go with him.

Amid the vast indifference of the black cliffs
the cluck of the dimpled surface
just past the tip of a submerged rock.

The earth flexes and degrades.
Man progresses.
"Portage yourself, Cap!"

Captain Walter Powell followed
his brother Wes, the Major,
to war.

Served under his brother's command
in Battery F, Second Illinois
Light Artillery.

And saw a rebel minié ball shatter
his brother's upraised hand,
gouging a bloody trench from wrist to elbow.

Inherited the command of Battery F
but could not believe in his authority
to risk men's lives,

could not discover wisdom
or even simple expedience
in his own orders.

Of the eighty-three men entrusted to his care,
forty-one were lost:
                    Porter, a minié ball in the eye socket,
                    Campbell, arms filled with his own intestines,
                    etcetera, etcetera . . .

And lived in fear of being shot by his own men,
half-thinking that he deserved it.
Captured at Atlanta.

Sent to Camp Sorghum, S.C., where, nothing to eat,
he ate grass until he vomited,
then ate his vomit.

Dysentery, fever, hard labor, rags on the feet.
Private Charles Carry Elliot,
native of Holly Springs, Miss.,

knocked him down with a musket butt, said:
"Get up, you damn devil!"
And raped him in the shade of a copper beech.

Shoved a gun muzzle in his mouth. "Yankee scum,
now I'm gonna give you what you deserve."
Click.

Click.
"Heh, heh, heh!
You're gonna remember me awhile, ain't you?"

March 1, 1865, turned over to the care of his brothers,
Wes and Bram.
"Thin as a skeleton," wrote Wes.

". . . moody and disagreeable. I am afraid
that Walter will be entirely unsuited for work
as a teacher."

Just past the tip of a submerged rock,
the cluck of the dimpled surface.

The suck as the oar
lifts out of the crinkled mirror

leaving a trail of drips.
Mass, momentum, and time.

〰〰〰〰〰

August 15, 1869
Once we got started we couldn't stop. The river was completely
unmanageable, sucking us down sluices, flinging us against
walls, whirling us in eddies, so that we had to row like demons
to get out. It just went on and on like this, and we couldn't
maintain any kind of order among our three boats. The Major,
in the *Emma Dean*, kept waving his flag, but so damn frantically
it was impossible to tell which way he wanted us to go. I don't
think he knew himself. It was every boat for itself and Devil
take the rest.

Shortly before noon we entered onto a stretch of mirror-
smooth water, let our oars go slack, and just drifted. After only
a few moments, however, the pace of the current began to
quicken and we heard—or rather felt—the first low rumblings
of approaching turbulence. Rounding a bend we saw the
mirror dip and shatter over the worst fall of the day. The *Maid*
had already been sucked into it and the *Emma Dean* was
hanging right on the racing edge. As soon as he saw us, the
Major thrust his flag toward the shore, indicating that we
should land and make a portage. We were still quite far above
the fall but, even so, we had to pull with all our might against
the current. As our bow skidded into a sort of cove, Captain
Powell leapt ashore and started running across the rocks.
Seneca Howland, who'd been having his turn as draftsman,
muttered something to me, then shouted: "Cap, come on back.
We're gonna run it." Of course, this was just the sort of thing
that would set the Captain off, and Seneca damn well knew it.
The Captain stopped in his tracks and said, "No. We can make
an easy portage here, right along the wall."

"The others have made it," Seneca shouted back. "It'll be a
pony ride."

I saw that he was right. The *Emma Dean* and the *Maid* had
both passed over the falls unharmed and were waiting for us in
calm water.

The Captain plunged his fists down and roared: "I'm the commander of this boat and I say we make a portage!"

Without so much as a nod to me, Seneca muttered, "Portage yourself, Cap!" and pushed off the rock with his oar, sending the boat arcing backward into the fast water. I was so astonished that I didn't even notice the Captain until he'd crashed like a meteor into the center of the boat. He went straight for Seneca's throat and might well have strangled him, had not the force of his landing sent our stern wheeling around on the sucking current. In the next instant we were going over the falls backward. At the bottom of a shoot our stern skidded off the slope of a great reflex wave, turning us broadside, just in time for the wave to crash over our heads. Breaker after breaker overwhelmed us. My oar was wrenched from my hands and all at once I was in the water, the firm muscle of the current flexing against my back. I went down into a roaring blackness, where pebbles swarmed like bees. My face emerged briefly on the wildly tilting and shattering surface. Another roar and a plunge. I went down head first this time, my legs having been swept out from under me by a rock, and I swallowed a good deal of the silty water. For a while I thought I was drowned, but then the buffeting and crashing ended and I felt myself surging forward into calmer water. I was nudged from behind by something hard, which I soon discovered was our battered *Sister*, drifting belly up. I flung my arm across her splintery hull and grabbed hold of the keel. A moment later I was joined by Seneca Howland. Now I too wanted to strangle him, but I barely had the strength to keep my head out of the water. Both of us lay gasping against the frayed wood until we heard shouting from the shore. Oramel Howland and the Major were calling for their brothers. Seneca was too weak to shout back. I couldn't see the Captain anywhere. I had time enough to think that maybe it wouldn't be so bad if we were to lose him, when the boat lurched and another set of fingers gripped the keel from the far side.

Once we'd paddled ashore, our comrades expressed their relief at our escape with a great round of hilarity. I had no stomach for it and just looked up the river, trying to retrace our path. Seneca explained that the reason we didn't make a portage was that we couldn't find a secure foothold. The

Captain never contradicted a word of his story. I'm not sure he
even heard it. He just walked away from the shore and sat
down on a beached log. I didn't say anything either.

The *Sister* seems to have weathered her tumble with only a
few more scuffs, but we'll have to spend tomorrow making
new oars. The flour got another drenching. No doubt it will be
flourishing with mold by morning.

Wes Powell, the Major, son of an itinerant preacher,
geologist, anthropologist, one-armed,
good for nothing

when there was hard work to be done,
left his men splitting a pine log
into quarters,

hacking the quarters down into oars,
whittling the white woodflesh down
until it was smoother

than the handflesh that would grip it
and more sweet,
and walked up a clear creek, or river

as it would be termed in this Western country,
which he had named "Bright Angel"
to counterbalance

a filthy flow of sulfur-stench, dubbed
"Dirty Devil" three weeks earlier,
before the granite,

when there was not so much need
to find beauty amid the flex
and degradation

of this earth.
First man
to navigate the Colorado

through the last hiatus on the map
of these American states
and territories,

climbed a red gully half a mile
out of the black granite
above the silty river,

drunk
with his aloneness
amid the enormous calm

of geologic time (shreds of cloud wheeled
from behind cliffs
to hang like sad balloons

over the layers of rusty sandstone,
greenish shale, and
granite),

followed an ancient trail,
worn into the rock
by generations of bare

feet, to the foundations
of a village
long abandoned by the Moqui

People, the Anasazi, who
retreated to the very edge
of the world,

banked their fields out
over emptiness
and disappeared,

at the hands of the armored
Spanish, or so Powell believed.
"The old Spanish conquerors

who had a monstrous greed
for gold and a wonderful lust
for saving souls," wrote Powell,

whose father carried
the message of grace to the churchless
in Ohio and Wisconsin,

the Spanish, who offered a choice:
"Be baptized or be hanged,
damned heathen!"

wrote Powell,
who believed that social evolution
proceeded from barbarism

to civilization.
Man of science, first to recognize
that land forms

are a record of the past,
first to seek the unrecorded history
of the Indians

in their speech and habits,
stroked the smooth depression,
soft as childflesh,

of a Moqui mealing stone,
and looked out under the weighty clouds,
at the grand erosion,

confirmation of his theories,
tranquil grave
of a murdered race,

and thought: It must be true
that this world is nothing
but time, matter, and force

because if there were justice
in Nature, then why
would she reward us

with survival?

. . .

Whereas the Navaho, believing
their ancestors were the ones
who vanquished the Moqui

by driving them into the Colorado,
where their souls found refuge
in the bodies of fish,

refused to eat fish
from that river, believing
that the past was not fixed

but malleable,
that present penance could undo
past sins, that self-

denial could restore
a human softness
to the hardness of rock

and history. And thus,
by this very gesture
of atonement,

they vanquished the Moqui
once again, whose flesh
they now detested,

whose smell and
appearance nauseated them,
poisoned by the indifference

of the earth
and the human
heart.

~~~~~~~

August 17, 1869
Disaster. This morning, while Rhodes was setting up to make
breakfast, he accidentally kicked the tin of saleratus into the
river, and all of it flowed away in a long white cloud before he
could fish the tin back out. This meant our biscuits were
tougher than some plates I've eaten off of, and a damnsight
more moldy. It'll be the same from here on in, I guess. The
Major gave Rhodes one of those long quiet looks of his. I was
waiting for him to explode, the way he did when Billy Dunn
drowned that high-priced chronometer, but all he said was,
very quietly, "We can't afford to make mistakes, Rhodes."
After lunch he had Andy Hall and Rhodes tally up how many
days of food we have left. Ten days of moldy flour, about as
many of dried apples, and enough coffee to last until Christmas. They decided, and all agreed, that the bacon was just too
rotten to eat, so we gave it a proper naval funeral. I can't say I
was sorry to see it go. I haven't taken a bite of it in days.
Nevertheless, I felt a hollow opening up in my stomach as I
watched it float away. *Ten days.* The Major says that's plenty of
time to get to the Rio Virgin, where there is a Mormon
settlement. Oramel Howland, who's been doing the maps, said
ten days isn't enough if the river keeps winding around like it's
been. For myself, I don't know. I'm not going to dwell on it.
The fact is, I think Oramel *wants* the food to run out. I think
he's sorry he ever came along with the Major and is looking for
an excuse to quit. Jack Sumner says if we tried to climb out of
the canyon here, we'd have 100 miles of bone-dry Apache and
Havasupi country before we reached a settlement. We made ten
or eleven miles today. Mostly rain, but every now and then there
was some sun. Strong sun! The thermometers went up to 115°
when the clouds broke, then down to 68° when they closed over
again. But it felt much, much colder. I've got a chill now. My
clothes are still drenched. And I haven't had my blanket since
Disaster Falls. Jack lets me have a corner of his. But only a corner.
"Nothing personal, Bradley," he says, "but if we were out in the
desert with only one canteen, I wouldn't let you have a drop."

Sometimes our exhaustion has advantages,
allowing us to work like machines,
                    knowing only what we see and feel:
the flex of our thighs,
                    the plunge and back-drift of our hands,
the oar blade skimming over the smooth surface,
                    and nothing more;
a peace in the skull that is like the reduction of all numbers
to one,
       or none,
not the first stroke,
                    not the eighty-sixth day,
                                   not the last,
a neglect of distinction that could be a revelation
were it not itself neglected,
                    a whiteness, and in that whiteness,
motion,
       a burning in the hands,
                    salt on the lips
and perhaps one thought: *We are accomplishing something*,
which is, after all,
                    what we were made for:
                                   not to reach the end
                                          of pain,
not to be treated fairly,
                    not to exalt at the pinnacle of creation,
but to be a force in the world,
                    a disruption.

━━━━━━

August 19, 1869
Glorious day! Hard portages in the morning, then endless
eddies spinning us about. But sunlight all afternoon. And now
stars! Straight overhead; some of them breaking loose and
making green blazes across the heavens. And best of all, a huge
fire, to warm my back and dry my clothes. It's amazing what a
dry shirt will do for the soul.

                    A simple impulse
          to draw it all
                    into his breast . . .

～～～～～

Jack Sumner: (Sotto voce) Here we go again, inspirational geology!

Major John Wesley Powell: Through the windows of these walls
          we may look
Back unnumbered centuries to when this place
Was the bed of an ancient ocean. Here coral
Animals built their reefs, lowly beings
Wrapped themselves in nacre shrouds, and unknown
Monsters of the deep lived, died, and were entombed
Upon the heaping remnants of their race
And their competitors, becoming stone ghosts of
          themselves,
Until a current in the earth lifted the sea bed
Into the open air, rupturing the rock,
Flinging ragged mountains many miles
Into the sky, and pouring lava oceans forth
From crevices and fissures. Mighty as these geologic forces
Were, hard as this stone, it is a fact
Of Nature that the strongest forces are most subtle.
Hard rock could not resist the gentle
Assault of air, of snowflake, and of rain. By
A process unimaginably slow, but relentless, mountains
Higher than any seen by man were pulverized,
Washed and blown away until the restless
Sea reclaimed its home. Three times
This land has lain beneath the sea, three
Times has it been lifted high and dry,
Three times have the rocks fractured and jets
Of lava shot into the air, three times
Have the golden, purple, and black hosts
Of heaven gathered over the rocks and carved
Out valleys with their storms. These mountains are
          minutiae,
Temporary and transient, younger even than
This river. When the earth last began
To buckle and upthrust, this already ancient flow
Cut the rising stone like a saw. Had
The land risen any faster or slower, had
The river been more slack or full, these canyons never

Would have formed. They are true miracles, the product
Of an all but impossible balance of natural forces.
The Lord has provided us with no greater
Wonders than those revealed in this book
Of stone. Not the stories of mile-high
Falls, nor of the river's plunge under-
Ground, with which the ignorant tried to dissuade
Us from our voyage, can surpass the astounding
Precision with which the Lord here enacts
His will, a precision that, by the way,
Makes these lesser wonders virtually impossible,
For the Lord Himself must submit to Natural Law . . .

Captain Walter Powell: That's just damn foolishness, Wes, and
            you
    Ought to know it! The Good Lord doesn't abide
    By any man-made law.
Major Powell: That's not
    What I'm saying—
Captain Powell: Oh, I know,
    What you're saying. You've got all these ideas
    About rocks and volcanoes, but all you really want
    To prove—
Major Powell: All I'm saying is that the Good
    Lord is consistent with Himself, Walter.
Captain Powell: Well, all I'm saying is that you can talk
    All you want about the Laws
    Of Nature, but the rest of us know that
    The Good Lord can do whatever He damn
    Well pleases.
Jack Sumner: Speak for yourself, Cap!
Rhodes Hawkins: Oh, Lord save us all!

A simple impulse
                    to become a force
            in the world:

Science as the ecstasy of man's strength;
Awe as the ecstasy of man's weakness.

This is the story of Billy Dunn,
bum
and mountain man.

Buckskin Billy
never bathed, never cut his hair,
only wanted the respect

he deserved.

"When I first met the Major, I felt obliged
to disabuse him of certain peculiar notions
he had regarding the habits of animals,
his knowledge being derived chiefly from books,
whereas mine was from personal observation
of animals in a perfectly wild state.
Beavers, for example."

Billy was born
near Pittsburgh,

his daddy pulling wheat
and potatoes up
out of the red dirt,

shipping them East
as a colorless liquid,
whiskey (Gaelic:

water of life),
balm to mill workers
in New York and Philadelphia,

being cheaper to transport
and store
in such a form.

His mamma, sickly from birth
and devout, club-footed,
succumbed to influenza

when he was four.

"The Major, who never doubted one of his own ideas,
even when it was damn foolishness,
simply would not listen to reason on the subject of beavers,
believing they used their tails as trowels and sleds
when building their dams. As he didn't want to be troubled
by the truth, I had no recourse but to lead him to a beaver
village on a ruse, where he could see with his own eyes
that they carried mud in their mouths
and never used their tails except as sculling oars
when they swam."

His daddy sold the farm
when he was four,

staked his future
on a hundred cheap acres
in Minnesota:

Wheat again, black earth,
no rocks, plenty of water,
and holy to the Indians.

Every summer the Sioux came,
set fire to his fields
and gutted a dog

on his doorstep.

"It was the same with grizzly bears. The Major
believed that they must necessarily be gray all over,
whereas the truth is that they can be as gray
as a mist or as black as a wet log and anything
in between, mainly differing from cinnamon
or black bears in the fact that they cannot retract
their claws and so make poor climbers.
But I could make no headway with the Major
on this point. When we saw a gray bear,
he'd say, 'That's a grizzly,' and I'd have to say yes

it was. But when I pointed to a black grizzly
and said, 'That's a grizzly too,' he'd just fire back
'It can't be; it's black.' "

Billy's daddy grew right
peculiar

one winter, holed up
in the stinking cabin,
snow drifting over the roof,

taking comfort from potato
whiskey, not talking
for whole weeks

sometimes. Come spring
he didn't plant,
took Billy, nine years old,

to an aged aunt in Minneapolis
and headed East
to collect a bad debt,

never returning.

"It has never ceased to amaze me how educated men
fail to use good common sense in their dealings with Indians,
and Major Powell is no exception. One afternoon
when we were up on the White River
the Major set us to pounding stakes into the ground
for some sort of geological purpose. We'd got
ten of them in when a band of Utes came down the hillside
waving spears over their heads. I told the Major
that we had best pull up the stakes and head for the river.
But, counting on his prestige and good manners to protect him,
he just marched toward the savages and explained
that we were only conducting scientific experiments.
Of course, to the Indians those stakes meant just one thing:
farming; and our cakes would have been dough
had Jack Sumner and I not intervened.

Sending greetings to our good friend Chief Antero,
we offered to pull the stakes out then and there,
and thus saved the skins of our whole party.
Neither of us ever got a word of thanks from the Major.
I'm sure Colonel Fetterman's guides were equally
well treated."

At sixteen, Billy,
known as "Dunn For"

in Minneapolis, headed West
to make his own life,
shot himself in the leg

accidentally, and shot a rancher
in the face
for docking his pay,

built himself a cabin
in Middle Park, Colorado,
spent winters alone,

not talking for weeks
sometimes, trapped
beaver, otter, marten,

and mink, bringing them
to Jack Sumner's
trading post in Hot Sulphur

Springs, liked Jack.
Jack liked Billy:
Bashful kid,

but a good trapper, dependable
and a good talker
with drink in him.

They talked mountain lore,
war stories,
Indians,

and women.

"I know his type. The Major is going to claim all the credit
and he'll get it, at least back in the States, and he'll probably
think he deserves it: Conqueror of Canyons! But the truth
is that he's been saved from death a hundred times
without ever even knowing it, by Jack Sumner, Oramel
Howland, and me. I'll tell you frankly,
I wouldn't bother for most men, but as Jack points out,
the Major has access to good government money."

Billy talked and talked
about women, but the truth

was that in his twenty-nine years
he'd had only one,
a Uinta Squaw,

and then he shot her.

~~~~~~~

     More ruins
     flint chips
     lizards
     locusts

          A basket waits one hundred years and,
          touched lightly by Major Powell,
          is dust

               So many flies
               circling our heads
               like the thoughts
               of the guilty

August 21, 1869
Glorious day. Got going early in the morning and had a wild
run for ten miles through a narrow winding canyon. Every
hundred yards or so the river would cut sharply right or left so

that we could never see what was in store for us. Down sudden
chutes, then up the slopes of waves that swept high along the
black granite before plunging back into midriver with a mad
roar. Around ten or eleven we came to a steep falls and made
a portage. We'd hardly got back in our boats and picked up our
oars than the swift current carried us around a bend and we
saw, not the gnarled, dark rock that had tortured and threat-
ened us for so many days, but a gentle arc of buff sandstone
blazing in the midday sun. "We're out of it!" shouted Billy
Dunn, and cheers went up from all three boats. We made ten
more miles along a swift river. No more rapids, but the canyon
continued to wind about considerably, taking us briefly back
into the cursed granite. Tonight, sitting around our campfire,
we are like a crew of escaped prisoners, nigh unto delirious at
our freedom, but secretly worried that the law will catch up
with us.

> A great and wise chief, lonely, lonely
> because his good and beautiful wife
> has died
>
> wants only to lie upon the ground
> and rise like a white mist
> into the dawn.
>
> Ta-vwoats is coming on his long wing feathers.
> He claps the earth and sky together
> in his anger.
>
> "Little man, little man, you must crawl
> across the stony desert all the days
> of your life.
>
> You must make your life out of stone.
> Do not waste the water of your eyes."
> "I cannot help myself,
>
> great Ta-vwoats. I am lonely, lonely, lonely."
> The god's anger is sand falling from the sky.
> The chief's tears turn to sand.

"Little man, if you will cease this womanish
wailing forever, I will take you
to your wife."

The great chief promises and keeps his promise.
Ta-vwoats is splitting the flesh of his own belly,
which is the desert itself

and the western mountains. He is leading the chief
along a path through the split stone
to the land of the dead,

where the wind is as gentle as child's breath
and the earth so soft it caresses the feet,
where meat hangs in the trees

like fruit and the people are so happy
they no longer remember
their lives in the stony desert.

The chief's dead wife is running past him,
laughing. She does not even recognize
her husband.

Ta-vwoats is leading the great and wise chief
down the path split through stone
and makes him promise

never to tell a living soul what he has seen.
The chief promises and keeps his promise.
But Ta-vwoats has little faith

in the words of men. He is pouring a river
down the path split through stone
to engulf any man

or woman who should grow tired of life
in the stony desert and long to visit
the land of the dead.

August 22, 1869
If it is possible to be cheated by Nature, we were cheated today.
The river is supposed to run easy now that we are out of the
granite—that's what all that cheering was about yesterday. But
instead we spent the whole morning lugging our boats over
reefs of marble and by noon were still in sight of last night's
camp. All of us were in a foul temper, sick of the blisters on our
hands, sick of the ache in our guts, and sick of each other
too—after not seeing another human soul for two months and
more. Following dinner we had a spell of deeper, swift-running
water, and it seemed as if we might yet make some progress
today—until the *Maid*, with Oramel Howland at the sculling
oar, ran up on a sharp submerged rock. The Major was furious.
Stump arm and all, that man is absolutely incapable of acknowl-
edging a weakness in himself and is even more intolerant of
weaknesses in other people—excepting, of course, his brother.
He and Oramel slung curses and accusations at each other for
about a half an hour, while the *Maid* swayed back and forth on
the current, getting more and more deeply impaled. It was only
when Jack Sumner suggested that it might be more productive
if we stopped "discussin' ancient history and rescued the *Maid*
from her delicate predicament" that reason was finally re-
stored, though not for long.

The rock came straight up from the bottom like a dagger,
providing no level surface on which to plant a foot or an oar
and give the *Maid* a lift. Oramel, Andy, and Rhodes abandoned
ship, but even without their weight, and with all nine of us on
the shore tugging a line attached to her bow, she still wouldn't
come loose. Finally Billy Dunn volunteered to row out and
unload some of the *Maid*'s provisions to give her a little extra
buoyancy. The Major told Jack to go with him, which was only
natural since one man couldn't handle both boats. But for some
reason Billy decided to take offense, and walked off with his
head slung low and his eyes squinty. When he got out onto the
Maid, he tore into the tarpaulins like a buzzard and started
throwing things to Jack without even looking. As soon as he
lifted the bag of flour, I knew what was going to happen.
Everybody did. We all let out one great gasp as we watched it
sail through the air and land crack on the *Emma Dean*'s
gunwale. Jack dove for it, but too late. It plunged beneath the

surface and reemerged a few yards down, shooting away on
the swift current. Andy Hall ran out on the rocks and managed
to drag it up onto the shore, but it was soaked through
completely, leaking great white rivers. Half our food gone! I felt
faint with hunger just looking at the sack, lying there, bleeding
white.

It turned out that the sack was all the *Maid* needed to float
free. Billy, suddenly calm, sat down at the sculling oar and
steered into shore, looking the Major straight in the eye with
that sick-dog squint of his the whole time. Mostly I think of
Billy Dunn as an ignorant bumpkin and a coward, but as he
stepped onto the rocks I saw the mountain man in him, the
man who, according to Jack, has blown the head off of more
than one white man and a dozen or so Indians.

"You damn blasted fool!" the Major shouted, shoving Billy
hard with his one good arm. "That's a month's rations you just
wasted. Do you hear me, man?" He shoved him again. "We
might starve out here, all because you don't have the sense of
a whipped mule!"

Billy just stood there looking fierce, not moving or saying a
word, trying to bull it out. But after a while, as it began to dawn
on him that on account of his fool-headedness we really were
going to go hungry, and him no less than the rest of us, his face
just crumpled. He looked like some miserable street urchin
caught stealing an apple.

Billy's helplessness only exacerbated the Major's fury. "We
can't afford your damn mistakes anymore, Dunn!" he shouted.
"Go on, get out of here! Try your luck with the Indians. I'm not
going to risk my life, and the lives of my men, on account of
some ignorant piece of filth!"

I'm sure the Major was just blowing off steam with this
remark, but Jack Sumner took him at his word. "This isn't the
army, Powell!" he shouted. "Nobody has to leave against his
will!"

Before the Major had a chance to answer, his own brother
pushed him aside and grabbed Jack by his shirtfront: "Shut up,
Sumner, or I'll knock that stinking mouth of yours right off
your face!"

I stepped between the two men to try to make peace and got
an elbow in the gut for my trouble. Billy Dunn rediscovered his
vocal cords and unleashed a rain of curses on the Major.

Oramel Howland joined in, Rhodes Hawkins told him to keep
out of it and, in an instant, we were all shouting, shoving, and
finally exchanging blows. I've never known the like. It was, I
suppose, a sort of settling of debts, the natural expression of
three months of suppressed anger, frustration, and fear. But
that makes it sound too rational. It was more shameful than
that. It was simple insanity. By the end of it I was rolling in the
shallows with Seneca Howland, my hands at his throat. Billy
Dunn and Andy Hall were locked in a paralytic embrace,
clutching hanks of each other's hair in their fists. And Jack
Sumner was waving his Colt .44 in the air, shouting at the
Captain to meet him on the sandbar. The sight of that waving
gun muzzle was what finally brought us to our senses. All at
once everybody, even the Captain, realized what a level of
madness we had reached. Grips relaxed. Fists lowered. Jack
Sumner said, "Ah, you're not worth wasting a bullet on." The
Major made us all shake hands, which helped a bit I guess.
Then he and the Captain went off to geologize and didn't come
back until after dark. Now we're just sitting around a smoldering fire, disgusted.

> Rat corpse
> in a sheltered pool
> short fur
> > wafting
> > in the wisp of current
> skimmed off the plunge
> and tumult
> > > food for small black fish.
> > > My brother

may be a great man,
a genius
> or saint even,
> > but he does not realize that he is clasped
> > within the hands of the Lord as firmly
> > as his mollusk fossils are clasped
> > by stone.
> > > Black mouths
> > > kiss the decomposing flesh
> > > shower of short hairs
> > > rasping teeth.

                                                My brother
believes
          that by the expansion of understanding
          and by methodical action based upon understanding
          he can outfox God.
                         He raised his hand
                         to issue a command
                         and the Lord put a bullet in it.

                         ~~~~~~~

Don't know how I've ended up out on the water with this pack
                of odd cards and that one-
armed joker, who thinks he's a king. No different than the rest
                I guess. Thought I'd take my chances
in the West. Snake eyes up against the double six. Time to cut
                my losses and put that scared look
in Mama's eye behind me. Just couldn't take one more spring
                of yellow pus on black sheep lips,
stick legs twitching in the raspy grass, ruination. Nothing but
                wormy beans all winter. Don't know
where I'm going, just somewhere different, somewhere better
                just because it's different. Good-
bye, Vermont, frigid runt of the ruined East. Good-bye, damn
                Pappy, rooted heart and hand to that
rocky land. Don't preach to me about the virtue of lugging
                boulders through the mud, of splitting
wood. I'm different. I'm lucky. I can feel it. But nothing's
                different out here where the water
eats the rocks, with the one-eyed jacks and the suicide kings,
                back broke, blood on my oar handles,
and a hole in my gut bigger than this whole damn canyon,
                nothing to fill it up with but dough
pebbles, morning and night. Mama gave me my orotund name
                and her faith that the horizon
could not contain me, fought Pappy to get me to school
                most years, taught me to worship
at the altar of a better world and could not believe her eyes
                when I left my books and set out
for that better world, believing I could make dollars rain from
                my fingertips. Fear is what I got

those days on the road, bashed up side my head, everything
        stolen but my youth, and that too
sometimes, cold nights on the black grass under some wagon,
        or in the wood smoke and piss
stink of some Christian flop house, until I came to places
        and stayed long enough to see
the snow settle and melt, flowers die and lake beds crack
        and give up their last gasp of mist,
only to find that they weren't any different and I wasn't
        any different than those greasy-
haired drifters with restless hands and legs twitching even
        in their sleep, nowhere to go and
no reason for staying. Still, luck's a funny thing, gives you
        a fortune and takes it away the
same night, at the same table, with the pistol in the drawer.
        Can you read, Oramel? he said.
Can you write? That's all he wanted to know and I was up
        to my elbows in words and ink,
printer, then editor of *The Rocky Mountain News*. A bum,
        then "voice of the people." Done
my mother proud, but she was long dead and buried. Pappy
        didn't care and neither did I,
in the end. Too long on the road I guess, took away my itch
        to be somewhere, be something,
even to make dollars rain from my fingertips. White cuffs
        and cuff links, dinner with the
mayor, a woman (not a wife) to cook my supper and make
        my bed. Nights between clean sheets,
I felt like my Pappy, roots for hands and feet, head under
        a boulder. Can you swim? he said.
Have you got a strong heart? We need someone to draw our
        maps. Can I bring my baby brother?
I said. (Namesake of the decadent stoic, pitched his camp
        in my parlor, looked up at me,
eyes of our dead mother, teary with whiskey, said: You
        always thought you were so damn
better than the rest of us!) I'm bringing my own, he said.
        So here I am, flotsam with the
flotsam, tracking every mile and twist of the river, every
        spill and eddy. Nights I sit by the fire

and get everybody's guess as to what turned up on the table
        that day, trace it out on brown paper,
subtract it from what's left in the deck: how many dough
        pebbles, how many days,
how many feet above the Rio Virgin, how many miles?
        Never kept such close count
before, which is why, I guess, luck always seemed like
        one wild card after another,
Surprise! You win! You lose! Don't think about it, just
        see what comes up next, you're
ahead of the game, aren't you? But now I'm looking at
        the end of the game and I think
I'm seeing what's been true all along, that in the end
        we can't win, we don't have
              the hand.

~~~~~~

Just imagine a river of molten rock
Running down into a river of melted
Snow! What a seething and boiling of waters!
What clouds of steam rolling into
The Heavens! Such was the spectacle
That transpired upon this very spot.
Here the earth split along a line
Crossing the river. The land on one side
Dropped eight hundred feet, and through the fissure
Thus formed (or what geologists would call
A fault) a geyser of lava shot into
The air and poured over the canyon wall,
Right here at this falls, filling the canyon
Three or four miles upriver
And we know not how many down,
Damming the waters to a height of fifteen hundred
Feet, as we can tell from the traces
Of black basalt still clinging high
Up the canyon walls. But there is
No stasis in nature. Here we see how
The river cut a channel through the soft
Sandstone (the heaped-up beds of long dead
Oceans) around the harder lava.

And here, as we proceed upon our own
Journey, we can see where even
The crystalline basalt could not resist the steady
Force of the tumbling waters . . .

                                        My brother
                         gets wild as a stallion
              over the pungent backside
              of a mare
                         wild as a Baptist preacher
                         shouting Dam-
                                        nation!
                         and Sal-
                                  vation!
                         in the sweat and burning
                         oil stink
                                  under a tent
              when he talks
              about the great and desolate force
              of God's will
                         that now surely
                         is going to destroy us.
              Did he feel proud watching Rebel
              minié balls
              splash into the flesh
                                  of good Union boys?
                                  Or thrill
              as graybellied
              waves
                                  poured over a hill?
              Did he flush with power
                         watching young men
              stagger on the field,
                                  holding
              their guts in their hands?
Half rations
(which are really half of quarter rations),
              dark spots spinning
                                  with the gnats and flies
in front of our eyes,
a great musty emptiness where our strength ought to be,

> while the river stays strong,
> stays stronger,
pain in our hands and backs
pain in our teeth,
> while the river never tires
and confusion,
animosity
> never stops
the great and desolate
will of the Lord
> forever and ever

> Amen

———————

August 26, 1869
The land up above belongs to the Apache, the Havasupi, and
the She-bits, but since leaving the Colorado Chiquito we have
seen no evidence that Indians, white men, or anybody has set
foot in these canyons since Moqui fled a century or two ago.
This morning, however, we rounded a bend and saw a thicket
of cornstalks sticking up out of the grass on a small floodplain
to the left of the river. I can hardly describe the peculiar effect
this sight had upon us, or upon me in any event. It was so
unlikely, so unexpected, that it made me question the evidence
of all of my senses. Everything around me—and the cornstalks
especially, of course—began to shimmer with the possibility
that it might not be real, that it might be some sort of confusion
or dream. The effect was enhanced by the fact that the sun was
shining, the air was warm but not hot, and that we were in all
respects blessed by a beautiful day. Our whole company was
silent as we stepped onto the gravel shore. I had been light-
headed for days, but now I felt as if I were floating. Which was
the illusion, all those weeks of rock and desolation or this small
island of cooperation between man and Nature? The corn was
too green for roasting, but there was also a small plantation of
squash that had ripened to perfection. Without a word, we
pulled out our knives and hacked off as many of the squash as
we could carry, then hightailed it back to our boats and pushed
off, lest we get caught at our robbery. As soon as we got far
enough down the river to be safe, we pulled ashore, started a

fire, and boiled those squash to a mulch that I won't exactly call delicious, but which tasted better than anything I've eaten in many, many weeks. And for the first time in almost that long I ate until my belly could hold no more. I think I'm ready to rejoin civilization. As I write, the image of Grandma Bradley's Christmas table is hovering before my eyes: a steaming leg of beef, smoked trout, a huge, brown turkey so well-cooked it falls apart at the joints, sweet potato pie, apple pie, Indian corn . . . Oh my!

> They studied it
> like monkeys
> like flies on a cadaver
> they climbed all over it
> this dread wonder
> this silence that beat upon their chests
> beat them to their knees
> and they worshipped it
> with silence.
> Their study
> was a form of cowardice really,
> but it is all we have of bravery,
> our gift to the earth.

Name this, said the Lord
and He brought before Adam

> a beast that lit the earth with its sneezes,
> chicken-legged, nimbus in its brain pan,
> ocean-haired and blacker than the voice of the jungle.

> Trees leapt from the earth as it walked,
> boulders burst,
> mountains of air heaved from horizon to horizon.

> On each of its one hundred and twenty fingers
> were wings,
> feathered, brown, fluttering.

> The creek of pullies sounded in its breast
> and the chuff of machinery.

And in its eyes the sad suspicion of an infant
still bloody from its mother's womb.

Name this, said the Lord
and Adam named it

with silence.

~~~~~~~

August 27, 1869
After a mere six days we were back in the granite. And tonight
we are camped above the worst falls we have yet encountered.
The thunder of its pouring tons beats continuously against our
breasts. None of us will have any sleep tonight listening to it.
We spent most of the afternoon clambering among crags and
pinnacles, trying to get a view downriver, to see what lies
ahead: certain death or reasonable hope. At one point the
Major climbed so far out on a diminishing ledge that, with only
one arm to cling onto the sheer face, he was unable to turn
around and retreat. It did not do any of our party good to see
our supposed leader trapped and petrified for his life, especially
since it was his own damned foolishness that got him out there
in the first place. I was the one who rescued him. I got a couple
of oars and wedged them into crevices so that he could use one
to step on as he turned around and the other as a hand rail. He
was a pale and humble man when he collapsed into my arms.
Nevertheless he said that he had spotted a way for us to make
it, "with a lot of hard rowing and a little bit of luck." A fair bit
of grumbling went up over that one, especially from Billy
Dunn. The Major talked all through supper as if our heading
downriver in the morning was a sure thing. No one said a word
against the idea, or for it, but I'll wager that there'll be
considerable discussion about it in the morning. The Howland
brothers have been murmuring intently between themselves.
Oramel has just gone over to talk to the Major. Something's
afoot.

Democracy is not an ideal,
just a stop-
gap.

Leadership, partaking of the highest human virtues,
Wisdom, Strength of Will,
Compassion, and Vision,
is the ideal,
but there are no ideal leaders.
Democracy is our concession to
Ignorance, Cowardice,
Greed, and Stupidity,
and thus
is our soundest social principle.

He came to me, rubbing his palms on the backside
of his breeches, head lowered, but mulish
                              determination
in his eyes, said: "Wes, let's take a walk up this creek a bit."
Here, for months, I've been despising this man, a stumbler

through life, a poet, eyes on the shimmery surface, not
noticing the dagger under the dimpled swirl, not noticing
the falls, boat wrecker,
                    but as we walked away
from the water and the fire light, on the loud gravel,

I found that I loved him, if only because we were both
so damn scared
                of dying. I was proud even, when he said,
"Wes, don't you see, you're gonna get us killed. This stops
being science after a while, and starts being foolishness."

I remembered why, when I met him, his fingers black
with ink in Bill Byers's office, I'd taken a shine to him,
my heart went out: Head full of possibilities,
                                 distracted by every
brave or beautiful idea, exclaimer at sunsets, vibrant lizard

backs, and women, fascinated by everything and interested
in nothing, a child,
                 and the river would make a man of him,
or so I thought. And perhaps it has. The two of us alone
under the vast distances of the stars, I stopped being

a leader: "I'm not sure this ever was science, Oramel."
But even as I felt closer to this man,
                                    this humble voice
in the roaring dark, than to anyone on earth,
even as I agreed that our plaster biscuits might not last us,

that this falls might not be the worst, my determination
to risk the river only became more sure,
                                    not for the reasons
I used against him. I cited distances and altitudes,
talked probabilities and made all the concessions

necessary to establish my competence and sincerity, but
in the end it seemed nothing,
                                    mere conjury, a confidence trick.
And still my determination grew stronger, as if, stripped of
obligation to fact and rational principle, it could be more fully

itself.
        He said: "I'm sorry, Wes, but my mind's made up."
We walked back along the creek to where the others lay
under their blankets, black lumps in the tilting firelight.
He said: "I'm sorry, Wes. I don't hold it against you."

My goodwill suddenly gone, I said:
                                    "We'll talk again
in the morning." Alone in the dark, I squinted at the stars
through a sextant, hefted scrawny flour sacks: tried to
measure by the pull on my shoulder the number of biscuits,

the number of days, the units of strength;
                                    tried to divine
the likely course of the river: The next bend is to the south,
deeper into the granite. But what about the next? Remembered
that all these days of rain will have left pools in the desert,

that we are in the country of the She-bits, who are said to be
friendly to white men, that there are Mormon settlements
only forty miles away over land, but ninety downriver.
By dawn my determination
                                    had become a cold thing, an iron clamp

on my skull. As the others shrugged off their blankets and set
their heels in the dust, I said, "Boys." Not a wink of sleep,
not even the appearance of rationality. "You no doubt know
that Oramel and I have suffered
                              a divergence of philosophy."

None of us wants to die. Maybe none will.
                              "This is a democracy,"
I said. "I put it up to you." Not one of us was fit to choose
and not one of us did choose for even half a right reason
(Walter, because no one else can stand him; Billy Dunn,

because he wants to laugh at my obituary . . .). Still,
if we are going to suffer, it's better that each of us
suffers for his own mistake, and not
                              someone else's.

———————

August 28, 1869
Our party is going to separate. Oramel Howland, Seneca
Howland, and Billy Dunn have chosen to strike out across the
desert until they come to a settlement of Saints. The rest of us
will take our chances on the river. The decision was made fairly
peaceably, especially considering the history of bad feelings
between each member of the departing group and the Major.
Relations between Oramel and the Major were downright
congenial, in fact. After we finished casting our lots, they
shook each other's hands solemnly and then embraced. The
Major has given Oramel duplicates of his notes and a letter to
his wife. I shall wrap this diary in an extra layer of oilcloth to
help insure that it survives even if I do not. Having written the
preceding sentence, two more or less contradictory thoughts
have occurred to me simultaneously. One is that this morning's
decision has had a strangely morbid effect upon us. We've been
going about our preparations in complete silence, casting each
other sideways glances, as if we are a crew of condemned men
who have just chosen their method of execution. Whereas in
fact all we have decided is either to take a walk across arid
Indian country or to run a few more rapids, both of which are

activities that we have accomplished successfully many times before. My other thought is that, since this may well be my last entry, I ought to make one final summation of, or response to . . . what? . . . to all of this . . . everything: the last testament of George Young Bradley! My head reels! I don't have the time. And in any event, I shall no doubt be picking up my pen this evening. I shall not lose my mind along with the rest.

                    The movement of gnats
              in a beam of light
                            that drops invisibly
        through the clear, cold
                        air
                            of a cave
            pleases the eye
                    like the rocking of leaves
                                    in a soft wind,
        the swirl of water
                        around a stone,
                                the leap of flame
                    from glowing wood
              into smoke.
                              Gathering light
                  in vibrating wings,
        the cloud
                of gnat society
                                stretches,
                    spins into a knot
                                and diffuses,
        all at a twitch,
                    through some gnat command
                                and for some
              gnat intention.
                        Not random,
                              but shapeless
                flight,
        the gnats define
                the light's hard edges
                            by disappearing.

〜〜〜〜〜

We left our barometers, fossils, minerals, and some
ammunition bound in canvas between two boulders,
certain they would be washed away in the spring flood
but our boats must be light.
                              Also we left my *Emma*

Dean. She leaks from all seams and the starboard
gunwale is badly split. Even so, should the Howlands
and Dunn have a change of heart, she will offer them
escape. The three men
                        watched from a crag as we glided

rapidly beneath them, just grazing the rock. Hall and
Rhodes, with me in the *Maid,* pulled hard and we angled
toward the chute.
                  The surface sank, quickened, then
fragmented into voracious white. We plunged and there

was nothing but noise and speed. Our lightness in the fall
was returned to us exactly in heaviness when our bow
heaved and rose, splitting
                            the heaping reflex wave.
Cold water sloshed around our waists as we shot onto a

racing calm, but we were through! The great fall was past!
This demon of nature that had loomed so in the night
                                                    —gone!
So rapidly I could hardly remember it. We drifted a moment
oars up, then Walter, Sumner, and Bradley in the *Sister*

coasted up beside us. Cheers and incredulity: "Is that it!"
they said. "Is that all!" The worst fall of our journey!
Our moment of truth!
                      We pulled ashore, unwrapped a rifle
and let go a blast, that echoed between the granite faces,

surmounted the fall and, we hoped, reached the ears
or our departed comrades, letting them know

we were all right, safe.
                              For two hours we bailed, resecured
our supplies, and waited for the others, not neglecting,

I confess, to indulge in self-congratulatory glee
at their expense. Still, when at last we had to leave, alone,
we were sobered.
                        This was only the first of the several falls
we had spotted yesterday, and we were moving deeper

into the granite. We ran a succession of rapids and
falls until noon. After dinner we were in another
bad place.
               The river thrashed around house-sized rocks
in great frothing waves and whirlpools, then a fall

and below it, another. We rowed upstream and
climbed to the crest of a cliff, from which it appeared
that it was possible to land
                                at a rupture in the canyon wall
just above the fall. I directed the men to begin lowering

the boats as far as the rupture, and continued on my own
until I reached a high ledge from which I could see that the
rupture was actually beyond the break of the fall.
                                                    Hastening
to the others, I found that they had already lowered Bradley,

in the *Sister*, most of the way down the thrashing rapids
above the fall. "Pull him back!" I shouted as I ran down
the hill, "There's no place to land!"
                                    But all of our strength
combined could not draw his boat against the current.

Caught in the permanent trough just past where the river
sank and surged over invisible rocks, the boat swung on
its taut rope gently out, then suddenly back against the
cliff face, again and again,
                            while Bradley slammed the stone

with an oar blade to keep the boat from smashing. To draw
him back we would have had to lower him to a point where
the force of the river was less violent,
                                        but only a few extra feet
of rope trailed on the ground behind us. While Hall ran for

more, I waved my hat and shouted, hoping Bradley would
understand that we were doing all we could.
                                        But he never even
glanced in our direction. We lowered the line on the current,
but still he could not hear or see. With great composure,

as the boat drifted away from the cliff, he put down
his oar and drew his knife.
                        He had had enough of waiting,
of wasting all his strength merely to preserve
a hopeless situation. But just before his knife

touched the groaning rope, the boat's stern post
snapped, whipped back into the air, halfway to the shore,
and the boat began to wheel away on the sliding current.
For an astonished
                moment, Bradley, perfectly erect, rotated

with his craft, then heaved the long scull oar into the stern
rowlock, and pulling with more strength than I ever thought
in him,
        yanked the boat around until it disappeared,
bow-forward, over the falls. For a long moment he was lost,

then we saw his boat bucking in the white foam, drifting
broadside over a leaping crest, down into a trough, then
around behind the great rock dividing the lower falls.
                                                Nothing
but mad foam and the hoarse bellow of the river. And then,

at first seeming too small, the distance being far greater
than any of us had imagined, we saw something dark, spinning
on the spreading white: Bradley in the *Sister*, swinging
his hat over his head.
                    It is curious to me how the knowledge

that we might die can make us feel immortal, how the very
thing that last night filled us with despair
                                        now ignited a strange,
subdued joy. Here, we had just watched a man nearly get
killed on this barbarous plunge, yet, would it not have

detracted from the thrilling solemnity, we might have
fought each other for the chance to follow. The *Maid*
could hold only three,
                        so I directed Walter (because of his
innocence) and Jack Sumner (because of his knowledge)

to take the safer land route. Rhodes, Hall, and I pushed away
from shore in the battered *Maid,* making fine progress
as far as the fall, but a twist
                        in the flow, just as we shot
into the hurtling air, was enough to turn us broadside

to the current. We were overwhelmed from the rear and
overturned by a back-leaping mountain of water. All was
black, white, racing, loud,
                        and no air, until Bradley's strong
hands grabbed me by the collar and dragged me onto dry rock.

Hall and Rhodes paddled the *Maid* to the shore a few yards
down. All safe, only an oar and a rifle lost. We bailed
until Walter and Sumner joined us, ran two or three miles
farther and turned to the northwest,
                                continuing until dark:

and we were out of the granite once more.
No talk that night.
                        Hasty supper and sleep.

~~~~~~~~

Just past the tip of a submerged rock,
the cluck of the dimpled surface.

The sucking noise as the oar
lifts out of the crinkled mirror,

leaving a trail of drips.

August 29, 1869
This morning all the talk was of the others. Are they still wandering in the arid wastes? Have they reached safety? Have they fallen prey to redskin villainy? Of course, what we were really talking about was ourselves. Once more we have emerged unscathed from the granite, but we have known too many such triumphs to see them as more than temporary relief. The next bend, the next hour, the next day may well bring new dangers that will make all of our triumphs, all of our strength and ingenuity into nothing.

Mass, momentum, and time.

An early start, sun, and shouts from boat to boat, an easy slide over still waters, two or three rapids that
quickened
the heart just enough to break the boredom, and then we noticed the cliffs falling, the clenched earth relaxing

to welcome the wide sky.
By noon we were out of the canyon. They say that for starving men food can be poison, a banquet certain death. I think that our return to this humble and human planet (loud birdsong and unencumbered shifting

of the air) had a similarly toxic effect. (Mapped land. There, where the bank dipped and the water paled to yellow-green, was the mouth of the Grand Wash.) At least as far as I myself was concerned, my heart or spirit,
my animal flesh could call

up no joy, no relief, nothing but the memory of my first moments of release from the hospital after the removal of my arm:
Still flimsy in my knees and head, fecal stench still in my nose, groans still haunting my ears, Emma took me

as far as the hospital's wide veranda: "I'm sorry, my love, I've forgotten my shawl." A light touch on my shoulder,

drawing me back. "No," I said, "I'll wait here." Supporting
my weakness
                    against the peeling column at the veranda's edge,

the fresh air was too sharp, the white glint of the April
sun on the black sticks and thumb-sized leaves of the wood
across the way
                    was too clean. Perhaps it was only the natural
reticence of an ill man on leaving, however grim, his healing

bed, but what I thought as I stood against the column,
waiting for my wife, was that I had no claim to this bright,
strong life, that I did not deserve it any more than the trees
deserve the wind.
                    What is it that draws me to such extremes?

From that moment, or soon after, the faith of my father
seemed nothing but fear, or at best an awkward metaphor,
on the verge of losing meaning.
                    What is it in me that finds
the vacancy of pure reason more beautiful than love,

justice, or even mysterious intention?
                    I found myself
on the yawning edge of mere accident and leapt in,
believing my absolute weakness would become my strength.
Perhaps my brother is right: My shameful atheism

is nothing but self-contradiction. I embrace death
only because of my faith in my immortality;
                    I scoff
at my father's fear only because I am myself afraid;
and banish divine intention only to substitute

my own.
        The rocks and the river were unimpressed
by my defiance or my understanding. And my survival
in no way detracted from their magnificence. I had
grasped them with my vanished hand and only chance

had preserved me.
                 Our ceremony of whoops and back slaps
yielded, as the horizons fell, to meditative strokes
and splashes, each of us absorbed in solitary deliberation
with the past or future, until my brother lifted his rough,

low voice: "Let saints on earth in concert sing . . ."
There was indeed some small perfection to this structure
of human sound crossing the water,
                           filtering into the grasses
and dark trees, breaking softly against the yellow stone,

and all of us kept quiet, granting this sad man
                               his moment.
But when he started in on "Before Jehovah's awful throne,"
Andy Hall shouted out: "I'm just a damn Yankee way down
in the South. I love to kiss Southern belles on the mouth!"

And we all joined in, filling the wide valley with
a somewhat less perfect structure of sound,
                           our humility
outworn, celebrating our muscles, guts, fool luck, wits,
and other parts also. So lost were we in this gay ruckus

that we hardly noticed the first other
                         human beings
we had seen in more than two months until we had nearly
passed them. Walter lifted his arm and we saw a head,
a brown back disappear, a last naked child snatched

behind a rock. Such was our astonishment, knowing
that these rocks and trees looked back at us, that we
could not muster one word of greeting, nor even
comment among ourselves,
                   and we drifted past

this hidden, silent band in complete silence.
                       Some hours
later we startled a woman, nothing on her but a necklace,
at her washing. She ran through the hip-high grass
along the bank shouting (Jack Sumner shouted: "Come on,

we're not that ugly, are we?"), until she came to a rough camp,
   no lodges, just shelters of bent and tied branches.
More shouts, running, women, men, children, all naked as
God made them, and soon the trampled camp was naked also,

except for the first woman, an infant gathered into her
arms, a small boy holding her hand, and a large man wearing
nothing but a hat.
     Our bows squeaked and crunched gently
against the muddy shore, all of us stirred by a sudden

eagerness for human intercourse.
        Sumner and I stepped
from the boats. Bradley and Hall unwrapped their rifles,
but kept them below the gunwales. The woman retreated
as we approached, but the man stood firm, though

evidently much frightened. "Friends," I said, in what
I knew of Paiute. "Good friends."
        The sound of his own
language seemed to reassure him. The woman drew somewhat
closer. "Good friends need help," I said, but he spoke

so rapidly when he answered that the only word
I understood was "Towae"—tobacco. "White man near?"
I asked. One word this time: "Towae."
        "White man village?"
"Towae." As we had only the scantiest supply of this

precious commodity, Sumner pulled a sliver of soap
from his pocket, which they exclaimed over, man, woman,
and child, as if it were a slice of the moon, but still
they would or could tell us nothing.
        What does reason

comprehend but rock reduced to abstract principle: weight
and density; and water reduced to volume and momentum?
What good is rationality in the realm
         of intention?
What barometer will tell me who should survive

in the struggle for this wilderness? Whose god is most true?
Whose appetites ought to be sacrificed? And whose
satisfied?
          Sometimes I think that I am drawn to these rough,
huge lands because they are closest to the Eden of my

clearest thoughts, the world as it was before the fertile
corruption of desire and faith. Some part of me simply wants
to dissolve into God's wide earth and sky and never
come home.
          "This time they're white," Sumner said,

lowering his telescope. Three men, a father and two sons,
naked as the savages, up to their shrunken loins in the cold
river, a broad seine stretched between them,
                                        squinted at us
silently as we drifted in their direction. I leapt

into the water beside the father, bearded, gray hair curling
down over his pimpled shoulders,
                              and introduced myself.
"I know who you are," he said. "You're supposed to be dead.
It was in the newspaper. Bishop Leithead cabled us from

Salt Lake City, said we should look out for your remains.
Said three of your men got on the wrong side
                                        of the She-bits.
Weren't grateful enough, I guess. The She-bits found
them in the desert, gave them food and drink, and your men

said thank you by violating a couple or three
                              squaws.   Killed
them too, I think. The She-bits didn't like that. There ain't
a whole lot left of your men to bury."

                         ～～～～～

August 31, 1869
Tomorrow the Major and Captain Powell will return to St.
Joseph and St. Thomas with Bishop Leithead to investigate the
massacre of the three white men. Their identity is still only

surmise, but we fear the worst. The Major insists with great passion that even if the dead men are the Howlands and Dunn, they would never have been capable of the crime they are accused of by the She-bits, but I will confess here, in the privacy of this document, that I think he is mainly trying to salve his guilty conscience and preserve his reputation as a scientist.

He has asked me to come with him, and has offered me work back at the University in Bloomington, but I think that I shall go on with Sumner, Hall, and Rhodes. They plan to continue charting the river as far as Fort Mojave, and from there journey overland to Los Angeles . . .

                              orange flesh
of fresh melon
                    wet on the lips
crunch of wagon wheels on dry clay
                                        horse snorts
                    dog yaps
        stew cooking
                    and Mr. Asa's slim daughter
                    "Oh no!"
                    pitcher smashed
and white puddle of milk around
                              her
                              bare
                              feet

. . . I have always wanted to see the Pacific.

V

Then came there unto him all his brethren, and all his sisters, and all they that had been of his acquaintance before, and did eat bread with him in his house. . . .

Job 42:11

Rescue

~~~~~~

"You're not dead, are you?" I said.

"No. I'm not," she answered, lifting her head from the ice. I wondered how she could talk with her jaw dangling down like that. Her cheek had come apart where the slab hit her, and had been washed by the melting snow. Now it was clean, like an uncooked chicken breast, grayish-pink, clumps of yellow, bluish bone, no blood.

"I thought so," I said. "The others haven't moved for quite some time. But I was just looking at you and thinking, You know, I think she's still alive."

"Well, I am."

"Thank God."

"But I have to say I don't feel too good." She eased her head back down.

"Of course not. That slab of ice just came rocketing down the slope. You're lucky it didn't take your head right off."

"Is that what it was? I was wondering how I got here. The last thing I remember was sitting down and making a little seat for myself in the snow. I thought I'd just wait for the rest of you guys to catch up with me. And I remember this sound . . ."

"It was a sick, awful sound. I can still hear it."

"It was a ringing. Like from a dinner bell. But the ring didn't stop. It just went on and on."

We were both quiet for a moment. The blue light coming through the snow we'd piled up at the mouth of the cave got brighter. We were all covered with this fine blue powder, and then it got dark again. It would do that. Light and dark. And then it would get so dark that I felt like I had dwindled down to nothing, just some sort of vibration from a pick axe traveling through the blackness inside a rock. Going down into the earth. Dwindling and traveling.

"That was just the beginning of our troubles," I said. "Then a storm came out of nowhere."

"Really? I don't remember that."

"Oh, God! The wind nearly blew us off the mountain. And then the snow! If you fell down, it would cover you in a minute."

"I do remember it was getting cloudy."

"A couple of the others thought we should just hightail it back down, but I said we'd never make it. I said, Dig in here. We can make a cave in the snow. That'll keep us warm until the storm is over. But they wouldn't listen. They just ran off. Idiots." The blue light. The powder. Really it was very beautiful. But then I realized she couldn't see it. All this time we'd been talking her eyes had been closed. Maybe one of them was slightly open. I saw a tiny gleam where her face was pressed against the ice. I wondered if I should tell her to open her eyes. I said, "The others didn't want to bring you in here."

"Really. Why not?"

"Oh, I don't know . . . I told them we couldn't leave you out there. I told them maybe . . ." I stopped talking. I didn't think I should tell her the whole story.

"Well, thank you very much." She smiled, or at least she meant to smile.

"You're welcome." Something about her smile made me itch all over, especially in my feet. "By the way, I'm a bit embarrassed to say this, but I've forgotten your name."

"Oh, that's all right." Her smile became wider. "I've forgotten yours too. But I didn't want to say anything."

We introduced ourselves.

I said, "But I do remember that I didn't like you before. Out there."

"Me too. I hated you. I couldn't understand why the others asked you along."

"But of course that doesn't matter now."

"Not at all. I don't even remember what it was I didn't like about you."

"Same here." We both laughed. But our laughs were strangely muted, distant-sounding. As if the snow snatched away our voices the moment they escaped our lips. "When we finally get out of here, you'll have to come over for dinner. My wife's a gourmet cook. She makes incredible Indian food. And Mexican. Really. You can never find food like hers in a restaurant, no matter how much you pay."

"I'd love to."

"Great. It's a date. As soon as we've both recovered."

"I'd love to meet your wife."

"Did you hear that?" I don't know why I said this. I hadn't heard anything. After saying it, I tried to think back in case I actually had heard something. But no, I really hadn't.

"Yes. You mean that scraping noise?"

I listened, but all I heard was a muted moaning, like someone talking in a deep sleep. "That's it," I said. And then I heard it. "It must be the others bringing help. I was wondering why they were taking so long."

"At last." She grunted and tried to lift herself.

"I'm sorry I can't offer to help you."

"Oh, that's quite all right." Although the bone had burst the skin of her right arm, she seemed to have no trouble pushing herself up. As her face lifted I saw that the part that had been pressed against the ice was remarkably well preserved. She was beautiful. She had a model's face. Which was strange, because I'd been thinking she was hideously ugly. "Do you want me to help you up?" she asked.

"Don't bother. I'm perfectly comfortable."

"Are you sure? Your feet are under water. And it's beginning to freeze."

"No, really, I'm fine." I was a little angry at her. There was no sense wasting our breath talking. The thing to do was start digging toward the noise. But neither of us could dig. It was all too astonishing. We watched the blue turn grayish white, and then crumble. Rough, dark hands thrust into our cave. I couldn't tell if these were the two or three from our party who had gone down. They had their hoods drawn up tight, so that their faces were hidden inside rings of fur. They looked more like animals than men. I couldn't understand why they'd drawn their hoods up so tight. They dug and grunted and shoved aside the snow and didn't say a word as they hauled us out into the brilliant day. It was still overcast, but compared to the cave I might have been floating in a cloud of light.

I saw my wife. She was standing at the back of the crowd, but she wouldn't look at me when I called to her. I called again, but she remained silent, motionless, a few feet back from everyone else. Her hood was off and I could see her red hair shining against the blank whiteness of the snow, but her head was turned to one side, away from me, looking down. And her face was in a very deep shadow, so that I couldn't quite make out her expression. Perhaps she was tired. This must have been extremely hard for her, emotionally and physically. She wasn't much of a mountaineer. In fact I was surprised to see her up here. She almost never came climbing with me, especially in the winter. But of course this was all different. And I found myself shedding tears of gratitude that she had come up to me now. Which is why it was so frustrating that she couldn't hear me. Even when I was standing right next to her she wouldn't look around. And I couldn't quite make out her face.

And then I don't know what happened. They took us down. It was a very long way. There were rooms. And a whiteness. Down and down. And it got colder and colder. I was surprised to find how little the cold bothered me now. It was like an old friend. It tasted sweet to me. Horribly sweet. So I was glad, at last, to find that I had been delivered to my doorstep. To my home. And this time my wife was completely different. "Who is it?" she said from behind the door. "Me," I said. The door flew open and she leapt into my arms, laughing and crying, and I was crying and laughing too. I lifted her off the floor and we reeled around and around until I lost my footing and we fell into a heap on the porch steps. I noticed that she was wearing a black, strapless evening gown, with long black gloves covered over with silver bangles. She'd had her hair done. It too was black. "My, my," I said, looking her over.

"I wanted everything to be perfect for you," she said.

I started to introduce her to my friend from the cave, but found I couldn't remember anyone's name, not my friend's, not my wife's. They both laughed and introduced themselves, but I was secretly horrified. How could I have forgotten my wife's name? I began to worry that my experience would have some sort of permanent effect on me.

My wife had put candles, hundreds of candles, all along the living-room wall and set up a table covered with food in the middle of the floor. There were baskets of apples, mangoes, pears, grapes; bags of bulgur and buckwheat and all sorts of grain. There was sugarcane and corn and broccoli and carrots and several cartons of eggs. But mostly there was meat, plates stacked high with beef and lamb and pork and chicken—none of it cooked, everything was raw. There were pigs' feet and sweetmeats and livers and kidneys of all sizes, and even some venison and quail. All of it stacked as high as our heads, red juice overflowing the plates and the table and making glistening puddles on the rug.

I was a little disappointed that my wife had not bothered to cook. But not for long. I leapt at the table and started grabbing whole handfuls of fruit and meat. Covering my face with it, thrusting it down my throat. It was wonderful. I hadn't eaten in days.

After a while—I don't know how long—I looked for my wife, to thank her, but she was gone. I dimly remembered her becoming sullen, turning her face to one side again and stepping into a shadow. At first I could not understand why she had done this, and then I knew. It was my friend. During my first seizure of hunger I had seen my friend standing beside the table, tears streaming down her cheeks. It was because of her dangling jaw. She couldn't eat. And even though I was still starving, I walked around behind her, cupped her jaw in my left hand and, with my right, picked up a strip of beef and slipped it between her lips. It was awkward at first, but eventually I learned how to mash the food with her molars and chop it with her incisors. I would place a strip of meat between her lips and then take some for myself. And of course my wife could not bear to watch me hugging another woman from behind, helping her to accomplish this most basic of functions. And it was true: The regular, supple motion of the grinding and incising was erotic. And I had in fact fallen passionately in love with this woman. But that didn't matter, because I loved my wife infinitely more. I had never known that I could have such a love. It was primal and vast. It was everything. And she was gone. I wanted to run after her but she was gone. And I didn't know where to look. And I couldn't move. I was paralyzed by the awful thought that I might never find her and she would never know this vast, wonderful, and terrible feeling that I had for her.